DOCTOR DOOM

Ceci Jenkinson lives in Wales with her husband, two sons (who give her lots of ideas for the Oli and Skipjack stories) and two border terriers (who keep her company while she writes – and pinch her biscuits whenever she stops to gaze out of the window).

The Mum Shop won the shorter novel category at the Sheffield Children's Book Awards 2009 and *~mes Are Forever* was shortlisted for Waterstone's ~~~k Prize 2009.

For ~~~~~~~~~~~~~~~kijack go to:

Praise for Oli and Skipjack's Tales of Trouble:

'Oli and Skipjack have all the makings of a classic pairing . . . Ceci Jenkinson has an instinctive feel for her audience and writes with pace and humour.' *Daily Telegraph*

'Jenkinson's style is quirky and extremely funny and the pacing is brilliant. [*Gnomes are Forever*] quickly becomes impossible to put down.' *Irish News*

'A marvellously funny book. An array of weird and wacky characters – complete with weird and wacky gadgets – makes [*The Spookoscope*] a great book that both boys and girls will absolutely love.' *Waterstone's Books Quarterly*

'A high-spirited adventure . . . rollicking along at 100 miles an hour.' *Daily Mail*

'I rated [*The Mum Shop*] 10/10 because it was a brilliant book.' Elizabeth Rhodes, age 11

'It's fantastic! *The Mum Shop* gets my vote for the best book.' Kennedy Tookey, age 10

DOCTOR DOOM

CECI JENKINSON

Illustrations by
Michael Broad

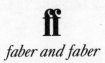

faber and faber

First published in 2010
by Faber and Faber Limited
Bloomsbury House, 74–77 Great Russell Street,
London, WC1B 3DA

Typeset by Mandy Norman
Printed in England by CPI BookMarque, Croydon

A CIP record for this book
is available from the British Library

ISBN 978–0–571–24970–1

2 4 6 8 10 9 7 5 3 1

To everyone at Packwood Haugh
and to the original Jack

THE GOOD
SPY'S
HANDBOOK

CONTENTS

Slugger Goes Batty

So this, thought Skipjack Haynes as he legged it down the street, is what Mr Bismuth means by cause and effect.

Mr Bismuth was eleven-year old Skipjack's science teacher. That is to say, Mr Bismuth taught science to everyone else in the class that Skipjack was in. Teaching science to Skipjack himself was not possible; it was like teaching ping-pong to a gnu. But one Scientific Phrase had recently penetrated Skipjack's head and that phrase was 'Cause and Effect'. Although this had been accidental (he *thought* Mr Bismuth said, 'pause and eject' and that a DVD was about to be played) he had listened for long enough to realise now that he was putting science into action.

The 'Cause' in Skipjack's case was that he had

fallen asleep during a cricket match. The 'Effect' was that Slugger Stubbins was chasing him through the town with a very large bat. The chain of reactions between the two was like this:

It was a Sunday afternoon in late May and God had switched on the heating for the half-term break. The town's cricket pitch was bathed in sunshine; insects hummed from flower to flower nearby and birds twittered in the trees. In fact, the only living thing in the whole park which did not radiate the joy of springtime was Skipjack. Why? Because the rugby season was over.

Skipjack was always miserable in May. Long afternoons spent waiting to be eleventh batsman, or hanging about in his usual fielding position of Boundary Grass Picker, made him yearn all the more for thrilling games of mud and mauls. Today was even worse than usual; no ball had come near him for about four thousand hours and now that Nevis Bullionberger was at the wicket there was even less hope of action, despite Nevis's brand-new £200 bat. Skipjack glanced over at a nearby tree whose freshly unfurled leaves cast an inviting circle of dappled shade on the sun-baked ground. Would his captain, Slugger Stubbins, notice a missing fielder? He doubted it. Slugger was too busy trying to bowl Nevis out and anyway he probably couldn't count to eleven.

It was quickly done. Skipjack stretched out in the long, cool grass and went to sleep.

Moments later he was awake again. The dappled sunlight had been blocked out by the dark bulk of Slugger Stubbins; the birds and bees scared speechless by angry shouts.

'Haynes! What are you doing under this tree when you're supposed to be at Deep Square Leg?' yelled Slugger.

Skipjack sat up. 'I'm sleeping,' he replied, surprised that this was not obvious, even to someone of Slugger's puny brainpower.

A rumbling sound like distant thunder came from somewhere inside Slugger's chest. 'Nevis Bullionburger just scored a four because you weren't there to stop his ball,' he growled.

'Oh. Sorry.' It was at this point that Skipjack noticed that his captain was holding a cricket bat.

'So we lost the match,' continued Slugger.

'Did we?' Skipjack scrambled to his feet and looked around for something to create a distraction.

'And I had a £10 bet with Nevis that he

couldn't score a run at all with his new bat.'

'That's unlucky.'

'So I lost the bet.'

'Don't look now, but there's an alien behind you.'

Slugger turned round. Skipjack ran.

And that's how he found himself pelting through the town with his mind on Cause and Effect. But time was running out; Slugger and the bat were catching up. Skipjack rounded a corner and dived behind a hedge. His pursuer rounded the same corner, and ran on.

Skipjack waited for several seconds before venturing out. Then he trotted off in the opposite direction, towards the High

Street and Doctor Levity's Joke Shop.

The Joke Shop was Skipjack's second home, so when he burst through the door with his tongue hanging out and his chest heaving, Doctor Levity didn't even stop juggling.

'I need a disguise, Doctor L,' panted Skipjack. 'Urgently.'

'What kind of disguise?' asked the shopkeeper, throwing five coloured rings higher and higher.

'A good one,' Skipjack told him.

'They're all good. You can be a gorilla, a wookie, a fishman . . .'

Skipjack stopped panting. 'What's a fishman?'

Doctor Levity shrugged. 'It's a fishman,' he replied, unable to find a better description.

'The problem is that I'm trying to hide from Slugger,' explained Skipjack, 'and he might notice me if I dress up as a fishman. Have you got anything more normal?'

Doctor Levity considered. Finally he said, 'I've got a giant chicken.'

Skipjack gave up. 'I'll just take this,' he said, grabbing a black wig which was attached to a false nose and dark glasses. 'Can I pay you later or, even better, can I just borrow it?'

'Take it, dear boy. I can refuse nothing to my best customer.'

'Thanks, Doctor L. You're a life-saver.' Skipjack pulled on the wig, adjusted the various attachments and slipped out. Making his way home, he tried to keep a lookout for Slugger but the wig was not helpful. Beyond the black hairy curtain which hung over his eyes, the world was a bit of a blur.

He was approaching his driveway and about to make a run for the front door when he heard a shout of 'Ah-ha!' and an extra big blur leapt into his path. Flinging his disguise to one side, Skipjack turned and legged it once more, while Slugger thundered behind him, just like a one-man herd of buffalo.

Skipjack was chased all the way back to the High Street, where he made a beeline for Mrs Happy's Pizza Shop. He fell through the door, locked it behind him and turned the 'open' sign to 'closed'.

Mrs Happy's real name was Sid and she was a round and cheerful person with bouncy orange hair who happened to create the world's most perfect triple-pepperoni pizzas. She was also a good friend to Skipjack and his best friend Oli Biggles and had helped them through many a tricky situation.

'Hiya, Skip!' shouted Sid from behind the counter. 'Are the police after you? Or just one of your girlfriends? Ho-ho!'

'Neither,' gasped Skipjack. 'It's Slugger.' He staggered over to a bar stool and collapsed on to it. 'He says it's my fault that he lost a cricket match *and* a bet with Nevis and now he wants to murder me.'

'He does look pretty cross,' agreed Sid, glancing towards the glass door, through which a fat purple face was now glaring. The door rattled violently. Skipjack jumped.

'Don't let him in, please,' he croaked.

Sid thumped him on the back with a chuckle. 'Worry not, Skipjack my friend. I won't let you be murdered. Not here, anyway – it would be bad for business! Ha ha! Now, how about a nice, cold drink?'

Oli Biggles had spent two whole days visiting relatives with his mum and both sisters. He had therefore missed the fateful cricket match and was unaware that his best friend was busy evading Death by Bat. On returning home that evening, he went straight up to his bedroom to finish making his periscope. This periscope was to join his growing collection of spying equipment, for it had long been Oli's ambition to become a secret agent and he had recently been given a new book which had rekindled this desire. *The Good Spy's Handbook* was stuffed with practical tips on espionage, together with step-by-step instructions on how to make various tools of the trade.

The periscope was nearly ready. Oli slid the two mirrors into their slots in the specially adapted milk cartons and sat back to admire his handiwork. With this brilliant device he would be able to see over walls, round corners and up drainpipes. It was time for a trial run.

There were three people in the house on whom Oli could test his periscope: his older sister Becky, his younger sister Tara and his mum. Oli's dad had died when Oli was small and at times like this he really wished he had a dad, because dads got much more excited about things like home-made periscopes than mums did, even nice mums like his. Perhaps Oli would show his periscope to Skipjack's dad at the weekend. He would understand.

Having ruled out spying on Becky because she would be doing something really boring like reading a hair magazine, Oli crept downstairs where he could hear Mum doing kitcheny things. He tiptoed across the hall, eased his periscope round the kitchen door and peered through the end. It worked! There was Mum, unloading the dishwasher. This was awesome. She didn't even notice she was being watched. As a subject for surveillance, however, she was not very exciting, so Oli crept away to find Tara.

As his mum sorted out the knives from the forks, she smiled to herself.

Tara was in the tree house, feeding her zoo. As Oli climbed the rope ladder he could hear her talking to her frog, Finbar the Third.

'Here's your grasshopper,' she was saying, 'and don't eat him all at once.'

Oli poked his periscope slowly up through the trap door. It worked here, too, only this time the result was not quite as satisfactory.

He saw Tara spin round to glare in his direction.

'What are you doing?' she demanded.

'Testing my new periscope,' he told her. 'In case I ever need to spy on an International Criminal Mastermind.'

'Don't bother,' his sister replied, turning back to Finbar III. 'You won't.'

Chalk and Cheese

Skipjack checked his watch. It was midnight. He rolled over with a groan. He had forgotten how uncomfortable Sid's sofabed was. When Slugger had looked like becoming a permanent fixture outside the pizza shop, Skipjack had asked if he could stay the night. He had phoned home for permission, giving the perfectly valid reason that he had promised to help Doctor Levity in the joke shop the next morning anyway, so it seemed easier just to stay in the High Street. That had solved the problem of getting past Slugger, who had, much later, given up waiting and trudged home.

But the combination of a mattress apparently stuffed with golf balls and the prospect of spending weeks running away from a nutcase with a cricket bat made sleep impossible.

Skipjack climbed out of his sleeping bag to check, yet again, that Slugger had not sneaked back to lurk outside. At first he thought the lamp-lit street was empty, but then a movement caught his eye and he was surprised to see someone standing on the doorstep of the dentist's house over the road. All he could tell about the figure, whose face was hidden by a raised overcoat collar and a pulled-down hat, was that it wasn't Slugger. As Skipjack watched, the front door opened and the visitor slipped inside.

At 8:59 on Monday morning a much more cheerful Skipjack emerged from Sid's place into the High Street. It was half-term, which meant no school for a week, he had enjoyed a fine breakfast of bacon-and-banana pizza and he was about to spend a whole morning in his favourite shop. Best of all, Slugger Stubbins and his Weapon of Skipjack-Destruction were nowhere to be seen.

Also at 8.59 on Monday morning, and on the other side of the High Street, a very un-cheerful Oli Biggles was staring at a blue front door which bore the name: Professor Vladimir Vakloff,

Dental Practitioner.

Oli's younger sister, Tara, had an unfortunate habit during check-ups of biting the dentist, which she swore she could not control but which had resulted in the whole family being banned from every dental surgery for miles around. So when Mrs Biggles heard that a new tooth doctor had set up shop in town, she was on the phone faster than you could say 'Ahh'.

And now here they all were, standing on Professor Vakloff's doorstep. Oli had a Bad Feeling about this new dentist. Nobody nice and smiley would ever be called Vladimir Vakloff. It was an International Criminal Mastermind's name. Oli had been thinking a lot about ICM's recently because *The Good Spy's Handbook* was packed with hints on how to spot one.

A shout from behind made Oli turn round. Skipjack was bounding towards him.

'Hi, Oli! Are you going in there? Bad luck. I'm off to Doctor Levity's. Come round when you've finished.'

'If I survive,' replied Oli. 'See you later, I hope.'

The blue front door was opened by a short, slimy man with a face like an angry puffer fish. 'Professor Vakloff will see you shortly,' he announced. 'I am his assistant, Plunk.'

As they took their seats in the waiting area, Oli kept a close eye on Plunk. His instinct told him that this assistant was Dodgy. For starters, he had a foreign accent which Oli identified, from watching lots of spy films, as Russian.

ALWAYS TRUST YOUR INSTINCT!

advised *The Good Spy's Handbook*. As Oli watched,
Plunk hastened to close a door that had been
left ajar, but not before Oli had caught a
glimpse of something very worrying indeed: an
ENORMOUS drill, with two great big handles
for gripping and a screwy bit on the end that was
as long as the sword on a swordfish. Oli gulped
and hoped very hard that he would not need a
filling. Next they heard a loud hammering noise.
Oli fought down the urge to run screaming into

the street, while his sister announced, 'I'm not going in there.' Mum glanced questioningly at Plunk.

'In between his appointments Professor Vakloff does essential repair work to the house,' the assistant explained. His googly eyes bulged at them and Oli thought that any second now his tongue would flick out and lick his eyeball.

The hammering stopped. Another minute dragged by. Then came an amplified click and a voice barked, 'Oliver Biggles to the surgery, please.'

'Good luck.' Mum smiled brightly.

Oli stood up and followed Plunk out of the waiting room and down a short corridor to another door. He could not rid his mind of that huge drill. He wished he'd spent more time brushing his teeth and less time just vaguely chewing his toothbrush. He took a deep breath and walked in.

A white-coated man was stationed by the big green chair. Professor Vladimir Vakloff was the polar opposite of his assistant: where Plunk was short, wide, yellowish and slimy-looking, the dentist was tall, thin and apparently made of chalk sticks. His long, bony face and his long, bony hands were as white as his coat; his eyes were sharp and his nose was sharper. Sharpest of all were his teeth, bared in a wolfish smile that made Oli feel horribly like one of the three little pigs. Two monstrous ears stuck out from  either side of his dark, stubbly head like fungi growing out of a rotting tree trunk in a dark, dank forest.

'Sit down, please,' said Professor Vakloff.

Oli gulped and thoughts about whether the dentist was really an International Criminal Mastermind were driven from his mind by thoughts about whether he was in fact a *vampire*. He climbed into the big green chair and spread himself out gingerly. He felt the chair rising up. The big square light was switched on, making him squint. He opened his mouth, closed his eyes and crossed his fingers.

Skipjack had promised to help Doctor Levity as part of a complicated financial deal. A month previously he had seen, hanging in the corner of the joke shop, a life-sized, glow-in-the-dark skeleton. It had been love at first sight.

'Just think, Oli,' he had exclaimed, 'not only will he light up the dark so I can see if there are any intruders in my bedroom, but there won't be any intruders because he'll scare them all away!'

'Why are skeletons always smiling?' Oli had wondered.

'Maybe they know something we don't,' Doctor Levity had suggested.

But there had been a hitch: Skipjack, as usual, had been broke. In the end Doctor Levity had agreed to let him have the skeleton in return for a couple of days' work in the shop. Skipjack had carried his luminous room-mate away, happy that he would never be worried by intruders.

But now it was pay-back time. Doctor Levity had called for Skipjack's help in the run-up to the annual Summer Fair, which was to take place the following Saturday. This highlight of the local calendar involved a fancy-dress parade through the town, followed by a jamboree in the park of Spiffing Castle, where prizes would be dished out for the best costumes. Doctor Levity was the only person in town who hired out fancy-dress so he always brought in extra supplies, until the little room at the back of his joke shop bulged with outfits of all kinds.

Doctor Hamish Levity was something of a mystery in the town. He had arrived ten years ago quite out of the blue, opened his joke shop, and stayed. Some said he had once been the legendary masked magician Cosmos the Magnificent who had toured the world, entertaining billionaires and royalty. Others said that he had been a circus acrobat and fire-eater. Most agreed that Doctor Levity was not his real name.

Even if you asked his granddaughter Daisy, who lived with him over the joke shop, she would only shake her pretty head and say she did not know much about Grandpa.

As for the joke shop, it was much more than just a joke shop. It was also a magic store, supplying tricks and props to magicians far and wide, and a museum as well, housing strange things that Doctor Levity had gathered during his mysterious past. In one corner stood a tall box for sawing magicians' assistants in half. Oli and Skipjack had examined this box from top to bottom for clues (and bloodstains) and had begged to be told its secrets but Doctor Levity would only smile and say, 'It's magic, dear boys, pure magic.'

In the small garden behind the shop was Doctor Levity's Home for Retired Rabbits, where bunnies who were long past being pulled out of top hats could lollop in peace until the time came to float up to the great dandelion meadow in the sky.

Skipjack entered the joke shop at 9.01 with a cheerful, 'Hello, Doctor L, hello, Daisy.'

'The sorcerer's apprentice arrives,' announced his employer. 'Welcome, welcome.'

'You're very lucky I made it today, Doctor L,'

said Skipjack. 'Slugger Stubbins spent most of yesterday trying to turn me into strawberry jam.'

Daisy giggled. Skipjack beamed. It has already been mentioned that Daisy was a pretty girl. Skipjack normally found pretty girls almost impossible to talk to, but Daisy was different. For one thing, she giggled at all his jokes, which was encouraging, and for another thing they shared a hobby: bubblegum. Skipjack was determined to break the world record for the biggest bubble ever blown and Daisy was the best bubblegum blower in town. She was his Official Trainer. She was also about nine years old and best friends with Tara Biggles.

'I'm afraid I've got bad news, though,' Skipjack went on. 'While I was on the run from Slugger I had to get rid of that wig, cos I couldn't see a thing. It felt like a Himalayan yak was sitting on my head.'

Daisy giggled again.

'But I'll pay you for it, Doctor L. You can add it to the skeleton money.'

'What if I told you,' said Doctor Levity, 'that it was worth a thousand pounds?'

Skipjack gulped. 'I guess I'll be working here for a long time.'

Doctor Levity smiled. 'Skipjack,' he said, 'you are worth your weight in golden fart powder.'

'Really?' said Skipjack, pleased.

'Really. Now, I must ascend my ladder to the giddy heights of the third shelf and bring order to the chaos in the Plastic Poo Department.'

'Shall I help?' asked Skipjack.

'Indeed you shall. You could start by telephoning the costume supplier for me. I hate telephoning the costume supplier. He has a voice like a Dalek. Or perhaps it's a she – I can't tell. I need a dozen monkey outfits, or rather Miss Green needs them, for the junior school show at the fair. The catalogue is by the till.'

'OK, Doctor L.'

'What are you going to dress up as on Saturday, Skipjack?' asked Daisy.

'I quite fancy the fishman,' he told her. 'Just in case it's a really wet day. Then I can swim everywhere.'

Daisy giggled. Skipjack grinned.

3
International Criminal Mastermind

Just ten minutes after Oli had been summoned to the big green chair, he was coming through the blue front door, into daylight and freedom.

'Well, that was the shortest appointment I've ever had,' he said, beaming.

'I didn't even have time to bite him,' complained Tara.

'Thank goodness that's over for another six months,' sighed Mum.

'Can we go next door to Doctor Levity's?' asked Oli.

'Of course,' replied Mum. 'Be home for lunch?'

'OK.' And off they went.

'Hi, everybody,' called Oli as he pushed open the joke shop door. 'What's new?'

'Welcome, Secret Agent and Amazing Animal

Girl,' called Doctor Levity from up his ladder. 'Elephant dung.'

'Elephant dung?'

'You asked what was new,' said Doctor Levity. 'The answer is elephant dung. Look.' He opened the largest of the boxes that he was trying to cram on to the shelf and dropped a big, brown, roundish object on to the floor. Oli and Tara looked at it.

'It's not very realistic,' said Tara.

'How do you know?' demanded Oli. 'You've never seen real elephant poo.'

Tara ignored him. 'And it doesn't smell.'

'You can buy the smell separately,' Skipjack explained, 'in a little bottle. You sprinkle it on. It's awesomely strong. We tried a drop outside and all the rabbits fainted.'

'Anyway, there aren't any elephants round here,' Tara pointed out.

'Exactly,' agreed Doctor Levity. 'All the more alarming to find a poo.'

'What else have you got?' asked Oli.

'A wonderfully gory new finger chopper, complete with fingers,' said Doctor Levity proudly. 'It's magic, pure magic.'

'Let's have a look,' grinned Oli.

Daisy turned to Tara. 'Come and see the rabbits,' she said and the two girls went out into the back yard, where they sat down among the pink-eyed whisker-twitchers and had a stroke feast.

'I'd love a rabbit,' sighed Tara.

'I'm sure Grandpa would let you have one for free,' Daisy told her. 'He only cares that people look after them properly.'

'I'd still need to buy a hutch, and food,' said Tara. 'Perhaps I could use some of Oli's Silence Money.'

Daisy's big eyes opened wide. 'Does Oli pay you silence money? What for?'

'He's supposed to go to after-school Dance Club every Thursday, but he skives,' explained Tara. 'He says it's embarrassing. He sneaks off to the rugby club instead, to practise kicking. Mum would be furious if she found out, so he pays me £1 a week not to tell. I'm saving it all for my Running Away to Africa fund. I've already got enough for a bus to the air –'

'Look!' interrupted Daisy. 'That rabbit's trying to escape!'

Tara turned round just as a little cotton-wool tail and two white tippy-toes were vanishing through a hole under the fence. 'It's gone into Professor Vakloff's garden,' she said.

'But he's so creepy!' exclaimed Daisy. 'He might eat it!'

'I'll make sure he doesn't,' Tara told her, pulling a chair up to the fence. 'You go round to the front door and explain what's happened.' She climbed on to the chair and peeped over.

'Good morning again,' said Professor Vakloff. He was sitting on the other side of the fence, marking off lengths of wood with a pen and a tape measure. 'Pleasant day,' he continued, as if he had fully expected a head to appear and stare at him.

Never one to shrivel with embarrassment, Tara came straight to the point. 'There's a rabbit in your garden, over by that bush,' she told him. 'Can my friend Daisy come and get it back, please?'

Professor Vakloff put down his tools. 'I'm

afraid that won't be possible,' he replied.

'Why not?' demanded Tara.

'He wants it for lunch!' squeaked Daisy behind her.

'The house is not safe for children, because of the building work. I shall fetch the rabbit myself.' He strode over to the bush and picked up the escapee by its long ears.

'Delicious to eat,' he remarked as he held it out over the fence. 'When I was a boy, my greatest pleasure was to shoot rabbits for the pot.'

'Murderer!' hissed Daisy.

Professor Vakloff smiled at Tara, showing his long, pointed teeth. 'Don't worry, Miss Biggles. I won't shoot this one, unless I become very hungry.' He gave a short, barking laugh to indicate that this was a Joke. Tara thanked him coldly, took the rabbit and handed it to Daisy. Then she blocked up the hole with a half-brick, while Daisy cuddled the poor little runaway who had so narrowly escaped the jaws of death.

When the girls returned to the shop they told Oli and Skipjack about their close encounter with the bunny assassin next door. Oli listened with interest, trying to decide whether this latest piece of information made Professor Vakloff more likely to be a vampire or an International Criminal Mastermind.

'What other strange things does he do?' he asked.

'He drills and hammers all day *and* all night,'

Daisy told him.

'That's strange,' said Oli.

'But you never see anyone coming or going.'

'Very strange,' said Oli.

'I saw someone last night,' Skipjack remembered. 'Professor Vakloff let in a visitor at about midnight.'

'Who was it?' asked Oli.

Skipjack shrugged. 'He was all wrapped up in a big coat and a hat.'

'It all sounds deeply dodgy to me,' said Oli with satisfaction. 'What do you think, Doctor L?'

'I can't comment on his dodginess,' said Doctor Levity. 'But he certainly makes more noise than our last neighbours.'

'Who were your last neighbours?' asked Tara.

'Funeral directors.'

'I suppose they had nice quiet clients,' agreed Skipjack.

Daisy giggled. Skipjack beamed, but then something happened to put out his light: The door was flung open and Slugger arrived. Skipjack ducked below the counter but it was too late: he had been spotted.

'Aha!' shouted Slugger. 'Here you are!'

'Am I?' Skipjack stood up again. 'Oh, yes. So I am.'

'I bet you thought I'd give up,' sneered Slugger. 'Well, I haven't. And you can't run away now. I've got you cornered.'

'I wasn't going to run away,' announced Skipjack. 'I was going to walk home, very calmly, and come back with a whole £10 note and give it to you to pay to Nevis.'

This news took a little while to filter through Slugger's brain. Everybody waited. Finally Slugger sniffed hard and said, 'All right. I suppose if you give me £10 I won't have to bash your head in. I'll be back in an hour.'

As he left the shop Oli hissed to Skipjack, 'But you haven't got a £10 note.'

'You know that, and I know that,' replied Skipjack, 'but by the time Slugger finds out I'll have found a new hiding place. Sorry, Doctor L, but can I finish tomorrow? See you later.'

For the rest of the day, Professor Vakloff lurked round every corner of Oli's mind. There was something fishy about that dentist. There was definitely something fishy about his assistant. What were they up to? The more Oli thought, the more he was inclined to rule out the vampire theory. For one thing, Vakloff and Plunk were both up and about during the day, which everyone knew vampires couldn't be without crumbling into dust. For another thing, vampires didn't receive Mysterious Midnight Visitors – vampires *were* Mysterious Midnight Visitors. And for a final thing, only teenagers believed in vampires. So what was their secret? As he lay in bed that evening, Oli reached for a note pad and pencil, found a clean page and wrote:

EVIDENCE:
1. enormous drill in cupboard
2. hammering and banging all day and night
3. hardly any patients
4. measuring long bits of wood
5. mysterious midnight visitor.

He stopped and chewed his pencil thoughtfully. He recalled more wise words from *The Good Spy's Handbook*:

ALWAYS USE LOGIC!

He chewed some more pencil and then he wrote:

CONCLUSIONS:
1. drill + hammering + bits of wood = Dr V is building something
2. hardly any patients = dentist act is just a cover
3. Plunk = evil henchman
4. mysterious midnight visitor = third member of gang.

Oli sat back, pleased. Professor Vakloff was definitely an International Criminal Mastermind. He was secretly building a prison in his cellar, probably so he could kidnap the Queen and hold her for a billion-pound ransom, or lock up the president of every single country in the world and take over the planet. All in all it was very lucky that Oli had learnt so much about Secret Intelligence. It was also lucky that he now had someone much more interesting to spy on than his mum and his sisters. And it was also *also* lucky that Sid's pizza shop was diagonally opposite Professor Vakloff's in the High Street. Oli jumped off his bed, picked up his periscope and ran down to the kitchen.

'Mum, can I go and see Sid tomorrow morning? I want to show her this.'

'What a fantastic periscope,' exclaimed Mum. 'Does it work?'

'Of course it works. I used it on you last night and you didn't even notice.'

Mum shook her head. 'I don't believe it. Any minute now you'll be called up by MI6.'

'I need a bit more practice first,' Oli told her.

'That's why I want to go round to Sid's. I think I'll learn more by spying on the High Street than by spying on you and Tara.'

Mum looked doubtful. 'I don't want you annoying anyone . . .'

'I won't, I promise. I'll just watch people walk past and maybe write down what they're wearing – that sort of thing.'

'OK. Go and ring Sid and ask her.'

Sid was delighted to hear that Oli wanted to set up his Secret Intelligence Headquarters above her pizza shop. 'That's smashing!' she shouted down the phone. 'It'll remind me of my days in the Ping Yong Police Force.'

So on Tuesday morning Oli packed all his equipment and *The Good Spy's Handbook* into his bicycle panniers and set off for the High Street. Fifteen minutes later he was knocking on the door of Mrs Happy's Pizza Shop.

'Hiya, Oli!' beamed Sid as she let him in. 'Come upstairs to the sitting room. It's got a great view of the whole High Street.'

Oli had already decided to come clean with Sid about the true nature of his mission. So now he said, 'I only need to see Professor Vakloff's house, cos that's the one I'll be watching.'

Sid's eyebrows shot up into her wild orange curls. 'Professor Vakloff, eh? Now why is he suspicious, apart from looking like an extra-terrestrial?'

'I think he's an International Criminal Mastermind,' said Oli, and explained his theory.

'I see.' Sid nodded. 'Well, you've a good view of his front door from this window. What method are you going to use to make sure you aren't spotted while you watch? I might be able to give you a few tips.'

'I've got this.' Oli showed her his periscope and she nodded approvingly.

'That's perfect. Just the sort of thing we used in Ping Yong.'

'And this,' said Oli, holding up a newspaper. 'I've cut a pair of holes through all the pages so I can open it up and pretend to read it but really be looking through from behind.'

Sid chuckled. 'That's brilliant. I can see you don't need any help from me. Good luck. I'm off to throw some turnips.'

'Onto a pizza?' asked Oli, privately deciding he would stick to triple pepperoni.

Sid roared. 'I don't think there's much demand for turnip pizzas, even in this crazy town,' she said. 'Nope. I'm entering Toss-the-Turnip at the fair this year. I'm determined to beat that great lump Herbert Haystack.'

'But Herbert Haystack hasn't been beaten for years and years,' Oli told her.

'Exactly. It's high time he was.'

She went back downstairs and Oli settled

down to watch Professor Vakloff's front door through his periscope.

It was an extremely boring front door. It opened only twice during its first half-hour under observation: once to let in old Mrs Higginbottom and once, five minutes later, to let her out again. Oli was willing to suspect almost anyone of being the third member of Professor Vakloff's gang, but even he could not quite suspect Mrs Higginbottom. He put down his periscope with a sigh. Would he ever see any Really Dodgy Characters?

Then he stiffened. Creeping up the opposite side of the street was a very dodgy character indeed.

4
A Very Dodgy Character

The very dodgy character was quite short and wore a long coat with a turned-up collar, a black hat pulled down low over his eyes, and dark glasses. Wasn't that exactly how Skipjack had described Professor Vakloff's Mysterious Midnight Visitor? Oli's heart woke up and started thumping. He watched intently as the stranger slunk along the wall of Doctor Levity's joke shop, peeped in through the window and then, with a sudden burst of speed, darted into the shop.

This was great news for Oli; Doctor Levity would be able to give him a good description of the stranger and perhaps even identify him. Then Oli had an even more exciting idea: when the stranger came out again, he could tail him! There was a whole chapter in *The Good Spy's Handbook* devoted to tailing and Oli was longing to try out all the recommended tactics.

But tailing the stranger meant seeing him leave the shop and this presented Oli with the dilemma of whose front door to watch: Professor Vakloff's or Doctor Levity's. For about an hour he turned his periscope from one to the other, like a mid-Atlantic submarine commander under threat from port and starboard. Finally it occurred to him that a whole hour was a very long time for anyone to spend in a joke shop (apart from Skipjack) and he wondered what the stranger was doing there. Oh, no! Perhaps the man had captured Doctor Levity and taken him hostage! Daisy too! Perhaps he had – gulp – *murdered* them!

Oli abandoned his post and tumbled down the stairs and out of the shop. Entirely careless of his own safety, he rushed across the street and threw open the door of the joke shop.

'Hi, Oli!'

'Skipjack!' Oli screeched to a halt. 'When did you get here?'

'About an hour ago.'

'But . . . but I've been watching from Sid's and I didn't see you.'

Skipjack looked pleased. 'That's because I was wearing a disguise, just in case Slugger was lying in wait. I got the idea from Professor Vakloff's Mysterious Midnight Visitor. Look.' He reached behind the counter and held up a long coat and a black hat. 'Good, huh?'

Oli leaned heavily on the counter. 'Yeah, Skip,' he sighed. 'Really good.'

'Why were you watching from Sid's?' asked his friend.

'I'm spying on the dentist. Because of him being an International Criminal Mastermind.'

'I hope he is,' said Skipjack. 'We could do with a bit of excitement round here.'

'Isn't the chance of having your head bashed in by Slugger exciting enough?'

'It was, but now I've thought of a way to stay unbashed,' said Skipjack. 'When Slugger arrives I'll point out that if he bashes me before I've finished working for Doctor Levity he won't get his £10. Even Slugger will see the logic in that.'

'Let's hope so,' said Oli. 'Well, I'm going back to my periscope. I don't want to miss anything suspicious.'

'I'll come and help you when I've finished here,' promised Skipjack. 'Perhaps Sid will give us some pizza.'

So Oli returned to his HQ and by the time his friend joined him a couple of hours later he was thoroughly fed up with Professor Vakloff's front door.

'I've brought you up some lunch,' said Skipjack, plonking onto the table two plates over-flopping with pizza.

'Good old Sid.' Oli put down the periscope.

'Anything interesting?' asked Skipjack.

'Nothing,' sighed Oli. 'I've only seen Mrs Higginbottom all morning and she was in and out in a few minutes.'

Skipjack picked up the periscope and peered

through. He trained it on the dentist's house, while Oli took a huge bite of pizza and munched thoughtfully.

'Here comes someone else,' said Skipjack. 'It's our new science teacher, Mr Bismuth. I'm glad he's going to the dentist – it might help his stinky breath.'

'Mr Bismuth hasn't got stinky breath,' mumbled Oli while he dealt with a particularly gooey stretch of cheese.

'He must have. He has a beard. Everyone who has a beard has stinky breath.'

'Like who?'

'Like my Uncle Devlin.'

'I didn't know you had an uncle called Devlin.'

'No one ever talks about him,' explained Skipjack. 'He's the black sheep of the family.'

'Because he has a beard?'

Skipjack shrugged. 'I think it's more than that. People always stop talking about him when I come into the room. I met him once, but all I remember is a great big beard. And stinky breath, which proves my point.'

'Not really,' said Oli. 'Name another stinky-beardy.'

'Mr Grimble,' said Skipjack at once. Mr Grimble was a local bus driver and the boys' Number One Enemy.

'OK,' conceded Oli, 'but his breath is only stinky cos he lives on onion pie. Anyway, even if Mr Bismuth's breath was stinky, Professor Vakloff wouldn't be able to do anything about it cos he probably isn't a real dentist.'

'Maybe Mr Bismuth isn't a real patient,' said Skipjack vaguely.

Oli sat up. What if the science teacher was

another member of the gang? It would fit perfectly:

1 x International Criminal Mastermind (Professor Vakloff)

1 x Hideous Henchman (Plunk)

1 x Mad Scientist (Mr Bismuth).

OK, so Mr Bismuth didn't seem any madder than all their other teachers, but that was mad enough for Oli.

'Maybe he isn't a real science teacher, either,' he suggested. 'Maybe he just took the job so he could be near the rest of Professor Vakloff's gang.'

Skipjack shook his head. 'No, Oli. He's definitely a real science teacher. He's got "I am a real science teacher"

written all over him. Plus he's got a beard.'

'Will you stop going on about beards? I'm not even sure if Mr Bismuth's beard is real. Doctor Levity used to sell one just like it, remember?'

'I bet you a tenner it's real,' said Skipjack.

'Done,' said Oli. They shook hands. Oli began to rummage through his bag of secret agent equipment and pulled out a glass bowl.

'What's that?' asked Skipjack.

'It's a listening device.'

'It looks like a salad bowl.'

'It is a salad bowl. But it's also a listening device. You put it against a wall and it amplifies any sound coming from the other side. That's science,' explained Oli.

Skipjack shuddered and said, 'I'll take your word for it.'

'I'm going to see if I can hear Professor Vakloff through the joke-shop wall,' Oli told him. 'You stay here and watch the house. If Mr Bismuth comes out, follow him.'

'Ooh, goody.'

For the second time that day, Oli ran over the road to the joke shop. Doctor Levity showed no surprise that his visitor wanted to spy on the neighbours with a salad bowl. Nothing surprised Doctor Levity.

As Oli placed his apparatus to the wall and his ear to the apparatus he only half-expected it to work. True, *The Good Spy's Handbook* had promised success, but Oli remained sceptical.

So he was even more thrilled when he distinctly heard Professor Vakloff murmur, 'Say aah.'

'Aah,' said Mr Bismuth.

There was silence for about thirty seconds. Then Professor Vakloff said, 'That's fine, Mr Bismuth. Your teeth are in perfect order.'

'Thank you, Professor Vakloff,' said the science teacher. 'Goodbye.'

Then Oli heard the front door open and close and soon afterwards the hammering started again.

What a boring conversation, thought Oli as he put down the bowl.

Or, was it, in fact, a code?

Constables and Costumes

The Good Spy should always, according to the *Handbook*, note even the most pointless conversations he overhears between suspects. So before Oli left the joke shop he took out his notebook and wrote down every word of the exchange that had just taken place between Professor Vakloff and his 'patient'. On returning to Sid's sitting room afterwards, he expected to find it empty, as Skipjack would be tailing Mr Bismuth. But the sitting room was not empty and Skipjack was not tailing Mr Bismuth. He was asleep in his chair.

'Skipjack!'

'Hmm?'

'You're sacked.'

'Oh, no. That's the second time today.'

'The second?'

'Doctor Levity sacked me this morning. He had asked me to order twelve monkey costumes yesterday but all that arrived today were twelve long, brown, hooded things.'

'I've never seen a monkey in a long, brown, hooded thing.'

'That's what Doctor Levity said. It turns out that I read the wrong code on the order form, the code for monk, not monkey.'

'So Miss Green's class will have to do a monk dance, whatever that might be?'

'No, cos Doctor Levity's ordered the monkey costumes now, but he's still lumbered with twelve long, brown, hooded things.'

'Is he cross?'

Skipjack shrugged. 'You know Doctor L – he doesn't get cross. He just said there wasn't any more work for me to do just now.'

'What about the luminous skeleton?' asked Oli.

'I'll have to think of something else. And there's Slugger's £10, too.'

'I can lend you £7.38,' offered Oli. 'D'you think that would stop him bashing you?'

Skipjack looked doubtful. 'He might bash me a bit less, I suppose. Thanks, Oli.'

They stayed in Sid's sitting room for most of the afternoon. Skipjack was very keen to miss the possible arrival of Slugger in the High Street and Oli was very keen *not* to miss the possible arrival of any visitors to Professor Vakloff.

As it happened, the only interesting arrival was that of three workmen in the middle of the road outside Professor Vakloff's house. This trio set up camp behind a barricade of traffic cones and road-building machines, like a tiny imperial outpost defending itself from a native uprising. Then they all sat down for a tea break.

When Sid came up for her own tea-break, the boys asked her what was going on outside.

'They're laying out a new pedestrian crossing at the top of the street,' she told them.

'Let's hope they make loads of noise and disturb Professor Vakloff,' said Oli.

'It would serve him right,' agreed Sid. 'When it's quiet I can hear his drilling and hammering from here, and last night I even felt the ground shake. It put me right off my turnip exercises.'

'Will you do your turnip exercises by the window tonight?' asked Oli. 'Then you could keep an eye on Vakloff's house for me.'

'I'll try,' promised Sid. 'But my turnip exercises are pretty vigorous so don't blame me if I miss something.'

The boys eventually went home, Oli giving Skipjack a lift on the back of his bike, which was very hard work for Oli and very uncomfortable for Skipjack.

That evening, Skipjack telephoned his friend with some good news.

'Guess what? I've got my job back.'

'That's great, Skip. I thought there wasn't any more work in the shop?'

'Ah-ha, but this time I'm going to work *outside* the shop. Now that Doctor L has twelve monk outfits to get rid of, he wants me to walk up and down the street wearing different costumes, to advertise his shop for the fair.'

Oli grinned. The Supreme Job Creator in the Universe could not have come up with a more perfect role for Skipjack.

By Wednesday morning, preparations for the Summer Fair were well under way. Posters and flags were up all over town, a crop of tents had sprouted in the grounds of Spiffing Castle, and miles of bunting had been strung out along the route of the parade.

Supervising proceedings in the High Street was Constable Bosk. When Oli arrived for his second day of spying, a banner was being hoisted between Professor Vakloff's house and the bank opposite, to mark the start of the parade. The policeman was standing in the middle of the

street, shouting directions to a pair of men on ladders about which end should be raised and which lowered, while the pedestrian-crossing workmen, whom he had shooed to one side, sat on the kerb and glared at him over their mugs of tea. But their mood changed to one of cheerful appreciation when the large and heavy banner fell down and managed wrap itself right around Constable Bosk.

Oli was so amused by Bosk's efforts to untangle himself that he did not notice another unusual sight further down the street. Leaning

against a lamp-post outside the joke shop was
a giant squid. And when this zoological oddity
spotted Oli, it came bouncing up, tentacles flying.

'Did you recognise me?' demanded the squid.

Oli saw that this was no time for harsh truths. 'No, Skip,' he replied. 'I had no idea it was you.'

'That means Slugger won't recognise me either,' said his friend happily. 'I hope he comes along. I could do strange, squiddy things right under his nose and he'd never know it was me.'

'He might guess,' warned Oli, 'especially if they were really strange.'

'Also, I'm in the perfect position to spy on Professor Vakloff's front door for you.'

'That's true,' agreed Oli.

'So am I un-sacked?'

Oli figured that even Skipjack couldn't fall asleep while walking up and down the High Street in a giant squid costume.

'Yep. Thanks, Skip. That means I can use the salad bowl again. If you see anyone going inside, come and tell me.'

'OK, Oli. Good luck.'

'Thanks. You too.'

But good luck was in short supply that morning. As soon as the rebellious banner had been firmly fixed, the workmen took up their tools once more and from then on any voices that Oli might have heard were drowned out by jackhammers and cement mixers. So loud were these machines that Oli didn't even hear the tinkle of the joke shop doorbell, so when a voice behind him demanded, 'And what do you think you're doing down there?' he jumped in the air and dropped his listening device.

The speaker was Constable Bosk, stout, red-faced and buttoned up in uniform. Oli tried to think of a good reason for kneeling on the floor with his ear to a salad bowl, but failed. 'I'm . . . I'm . . . ' he began.

The cool voice of Doctor Levity broke in. 'He's undergoing medical treatment for earache, Constable,' he said.

PC Bosk raised his eyebrows very slowly to full stretch, in order to demonstrate maximum disbelief. 'Is that so?' he enquired.

'It is. The bowl exerts a pressure on the ear which relieves the ache,' continued Doctor Levity, 'and, being glass, it is cool and therefore helps to shrink the blood vessels. How's it going, Oli?'

'Much better, thanks,' replied Oli.

The constable frowned, but he was no match for a bluffer of Doctor Levity's skill and he knew it. He changed the subject. 'I came to ask you,' he said, 'whether that giant squid has anything to do with you.'

'It has everything to do with me,' replied Doctor Levity. 'It's my giant squid and my employee inside the giant squid.'

'How old is your employee?'

'Eleven. Why?'

'Because when I walked past just now, he said, "Squelch, squelch".'

A spluttering noise came from Oli which Doctor Levity quickly covered with a cough. 'I imagine he thinks that's the sound a giant squid makes,' he told the policeman, 'and he was just treating you to a full performance. You should feel very honoured.'

'Yes, well. I've no doubt he's breaking several by-laws. But I came here on more important business. Please ensure that any vehicles you own are removed from the route of the parade by 8 a.m. on Saturday morning. Failure to do so will result in a large fine.'

There was a collective sigh of relief up and down the High Street when Constable Bosk finally left to arrange the one-gun salute with which the Mayor, Sir Henry Widebottom, would officially open the Summer Fair at 11 o'clock on Saturday morning.

Since Oli could not hear anything except banging and drilling through the wall, he returned to Sid's sitting room to keep one eye on Professor Vakloff's front door whilst re-reading, in *The Good Spy's Handbook*, the chapter entitled:

Tailing your Suspect!

The dentist had no visitors at all, but Skipjack did. Oli caught sight of Slugger Stubbins lumbering towards the joke shop, looking as grizzly as a grizzly bear that has just been through a grizzling machine on full grizzle.

Skipjack was jumping up and down in front of his reflection in Doctor Levity's window, apparently trying to make all his tentacles fly in the air at once.

Oli rapped desperately on the window, but such a tiny sound could never compete with the clamour of the road-builders. He could only watch events unfold with his fingers crossed.

Skipjack caught sight of Slugger's reflection behind his own and stopped jumping. Slugger was staring at the giant squid. Then he said something. Skipjack shook his orange rubber head. Slugger said something else. Skipjack pointed a tentacle in the direction of the joke shop door. Slugger frowned at him, long and hard, and went inside. Skipjack took to his heels (all twelve of them) and raced across the road.

A moment later he came thundering up the stairs and collapsed on the sofa in a heap of giggles and rubber tentacles. Seconds later Slugger emerged from Doctor Levity's looking,

if possible, even more grizzly than before, and glared across the street at the pizza shop. He knew exactly where his prey had gone to ground, but he also knew that he didn't have a hope of getting past Sid. He would have to give up his bashing plan. For now.

Still nobody came or went through Professor Vakloff's front door and Oli became increasingly convinced that all International Criminal Mastermind action took place during the hours of darkness. So how was he to find out what was going on? Even if he slept over at Sid's place, he would not be able to keep watch for the whole night. And it was no good asking Skipjack to share the job – he wouldn't stay awake for five minutes. Nor was it fair to ask Sid – she needed her sleep to keep up her strength for Toss-the-Turnip.

Despairing of ever finding out more about Professor Vakloff's dastardly plans, Oli turned to the next chapter in *The Good Spy's Handbook* and his eyes nearly dropped out of his head when he read the title:

Alarms and Tripwires.

That was it: he would build an alarm circuit and connect it to a long tripwire fixed at one end to a spot near Professor Vakloff's front door, late at night. Then he would be woken up by any Mysterious Midnight Visitors disturbing the tripwire and setting off the alarm. He looked through the list of things he would need: a battery, a clothes peg, some fishing line, aluminium foil, a mousetrap, copper wire, sticky tape and 'a noisy electronic part from a toy'. Easy-peasy!

6
A Tail of Two Subjects

The easy-peasy task of building the tripwire alarm took Oli the rest of the afternoon and all evening, during most of which he deeply regretted not paying more attention in his Design and Technology lessons. He also regretted the day he and Skipjack had driven all his remote-control cars off a ramp through his bedroom window to see which would fly the furthest, as he could not find one car with an electronic part that still worked. Finally he dismantled his Talking Yoda so that, when the wire was tripped, the battery-powered voice of the Jedi Master gave out stern warnings about obeying the Force.

Mum agreed to let Oli spend the following night at Sid's, after making him promise that he was not planning to annoy anyone.

'But you'll have to get yourself there from

the school,' she said, 'after your rehearsal in the morning.'

Oli looked blank. 'My what?'

'Your rehearsal,' repeated Mum.

'You remember,' put in Tara with a wink, 'for our *Dance Club* performance at the fair on Saturday.'

'Oh, yeah,' said Oli and for a moment he was grateful for his sister's help. Then he remembered that this was all part of the service he was buying for his £1 a week Silence Money.

So on Thursday morning Mum dropped them off in the school car park. Oli hung around until she was safely out of sight and Tara hung around as well, in order to demand what exactly her brother was planning to do about Saturday's show. 'You can't be in it,' she told him with satisfaction, 'because you haven't been to any of the practices. And Mum will want to know why you're not in it, and if she asks Miss Green she'll find out that you're not even in the group.'

'I'll pretend to twist my ankle or something,' shrugged Oli, who was in a hurry to get to the High Street.

His first job was to find Daisy. He needed her help with the tripwire alarm, because Sid's place was too far from Professor Vakloff's to take the fishing line, so the alarm would have to be set up in the joke shop instead, where Oli would need an accomplice.

He arrived to find Skipjack helping Doctor Levity unpack a new delivery. On the counter was a big stack of £10 notes.

'Wow, Doctor L – I never knew you were so rich,' said Oli.

'Alas, dear boy,' said Doctor Levity, 'those are not real, but magic. Pure magic.' He took a note from the top of the pile. 'It looks like a normal £10 note, does it not?' The boys nodded. 'But peel this transparent coating off the front and the back and, in about an hour, the ink will have faded completely, leaving just a blank piece of white paper.'

'Forgeries?' asked Skipjack.

'Not exactly. You couldn't use them in shops because they're missing the serial number. But they're good enough to fool friends. And enemies, of course.'

Oli glanced at his friend. 'Are you thinking what I think you're thinking?'

Skipjack grinned. It would land him in more trouble than ever with Slugger, but it was irresistible.

Oli turned to Doctor Levity. 'Where's Daisy?' he asked. 'I need a little favour.'

'She's feeding the rabbits. As long as the little favour isn't a dangerous spying job.'

'Of course not,' said Oli. 'We want to do all the dangerous spying jobs ourselves, don't we, Skip?'

'We do?' Looking doubtful, Skipjack followed his friend outside, where they found Daisy scattering lettuce. Oli produced his tripwire alarm and explained how it worked.

'I'll tie one end of the line to the railings outside Professor Vakloff's house,' he said, 'and bring it past his front door. The other end of the line is inside this folded triangle of paper which will be between the two ends of this clothes peg attached to the alarm circuit. When someone disturbs the line by going through Professor Vakloff's front door, the paper will be pulled out and the two ends of the clothes peg will meet. They're covered with aluminium foil, so when they connect, it completes the circuit and the alarm goes off. Like this.'

He tugged the triangle of paper out of the clothes peg and, to Skipjack's huge delight, an invisible Yoda at once urged them 'the dark path to follow not'.

'It's awesome,' said Skipjack. 'You're getting to be as much of a mad scientist as Mr Bismuth, Oli. Lucky you're on the side of the good guys.'

'But what do you want me to do?' asked Daisy.

'I'm planning to use this tonight,' explained Oli, 'so I'll be sleeping at Sid's place. But the line won't stretch that far, so I want to put it through your front window, Daisy. What I want you to do is to sleep downstairs so you're near it. Before you go to sleep, you must make sure that the piece of paper is between the two ends of the clothes peg and that it's switched on. Then, if the alarm starts, you only have to telephone Sid's and I'll come over and listen at the wall.'

'It'll be a bit creepy sleeping downstairs,' said Daisy, 'but I don't mind.'

'I'll lend you my luminous skeleton,' offered Skipjack. 'He'll protect you.' But Daisy just giggled.

Skipjack chose the fishman costume that day – lots of bluey-green foam rubber covered in spikes and fins, with leg-holes and a matching trident – and spent the morning alarming very small children and little old ladies by barking whenever they passed.

There was great excitement towards lunchtime when the Mayor, Sir Henry

Widebottom, arrived to select his costume for the
Fair. Sir Henry brought along a photographer, a
reporter and two assistants and made a huge fuss
of the fishman, insisting they have their picture
taken arm-in-fin. While the photographer clicked
away and the reporter and the two assistants
laughed merrily (and so did Oli), Skipjack was so
embarrassed he forgot to bark.

Having squeezed every last drop out of this

crowd-pleasing scene, the mayoral party, followed by Oli, proceeded into the joke shop, where Sir Henry perused the rails of costumes. After much suspense he announced that he would attend the Summer Fair in the costume of . . . a monk. The reporter and the two assistants laughed merrily while the photographer clicked away. Doctor Levity, aware that there might be eleven other monks at Saturday's fair, tried to point out the benefits of being an alien or a snowman but it was no use; Sir Henry was determined to be a monk.

Skipjack had remained outside during the selection process and while he was leaning on his lamp post, thinking anti-Mayor thoughts, he saw something which made him quite forget his recent embarrassment.

Professor Vakloff's assistant Plunk was scuttling down the street! He had to be followed! But not by a fishman. Skipjack sprang to the joke shop window and knocked urgently, so urgently he nearly broke the glass. Most of the shop's occupants had eyes and ears only for the mayor so only Oli, whose brain was tuned in to things like Urgent Knocks on Windows, turned round. He saw the fishman's flippers waving frantically and came outside.

'It's Plunk,' explained Skipjack. 'He's gone off down the street, looking Dodgy. You must follow him.'

Oli's heart leapt. Now for some real spy-work!

He caught sight of Plunk turning left at the bottom of the High Street and hurried after him. Plunk (or 'the Subject' as a real secret agent would say) continued for a while and then stopped to look in a shop window. But is he *really* looking in a shop window, wondered Oli, or is he waiting to see if I stop, too? Oli knew all about this trick from *The Good Spy's Handbook*. He decided to walk on, resisting the temptation to peep sideways at the Subject, and he went into a sweet shop on the next corner to wait for Plunk to go past.

He had spent nearly a minute pretending to decide between a bag of chocolate caramels and a football magazine, and was beginning to panic that Plunk had gone along a different route, when at last he saw those googly features passing the window. Oli shot to the door and resumed his stalk.

But as Oli tailed Plunk, he began to have a sneaky feeling that somebody else was tailing him. He spun round once or twice, but no one stooped suddenly to tie a shoelace; no one dived up a side-street or into a shop. Oli walked on.

Plunk turned into the town park and Oli remembered that under his grey hoodie he was wearing an olive-green T-shirt which would provide much better camouflage. Also, *The Good Spy's Handbook* said you should try to change your appearance once or twice while tailing someone. So he stepped behind a tree and pulled off the hoodie, tying it round his waist.

At first the Subject took a path flanked with helpful bushes, but then he struck out across a big, bare stretch of grass towards a bench. Oli had spent hours practising his leopard crawl for just such an occasion but, even so, he dared not cross such an exposed area. Instead he decided to observe Plunk from the safety of a big tree. He remembered to check that his shadow fell inside the tree's shadow, and he remembered to remove

his watch so it wouldn't glint in the sun.
Then he peeped round.

The Subject had sat down on the bench
and was checking his watch. Then he took
out his mobile phone and dialled a number.
Glancing about to make sure no one was
within earshot, he spoke a few brief words
and then put the phone away before setting
off once more. Far behind him followed Oli.

And far behind Oli followed someone else.

When Oli realised that the Subject was
heading for the bus station his heart sank,

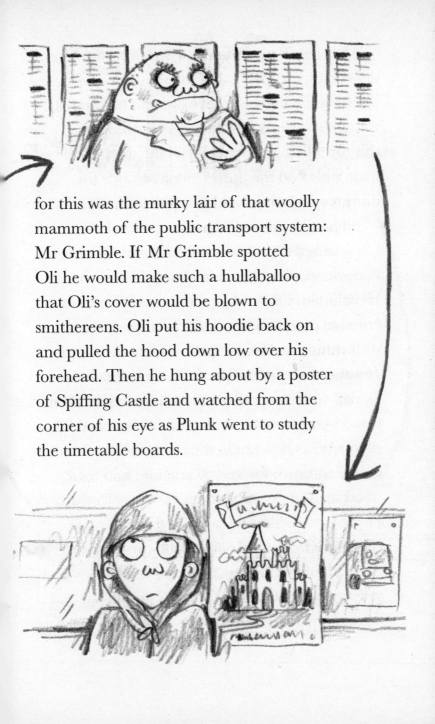

for this was the murky lair of that woolly
mammoth of the public transport system:
Mr Grimble. If Mr Grimble spotted
Oli he would make such a hullaballoo
that Oli's cover would be blown to
smithereens. Oli put his hoodie back on
and pulled the hood down low over his
forehead. Then he hung about by a poster
of Spiffing Castle and watched from the
corner of his eye as Plunk went to study
the timetable boards.

After about two minutes a bus drew up. Its doors banged open and a stream of people poured off. Oli would have thought nothing of this – he was in a bus station after all, where this sort of thing happened all the time – if he hadn't noticed the Subject look towards the dismounting crowd and give a slight nod.

But which passenger had he nodded at? Oli scanned their faces to see if any looked dodgy enough to be nodded at by a Hideous Henchman. Only one stood out as having real criminal potential: a tall, dark-haired man with shifty eyes. Oli didn't need *The Good Spy's Handbook* to tell him that shifty eyes equalled Dodgy with a capital D. This man strolled into a frosted-glass waiting room and Oli watched his silhouette as he went to the corner of the empty room, sat down for several seconds, and then stood up and came back out. As he walked away, Plunk hastened inside, went to the very same corner and emerged once more, carrying a *parcel*.

As Plunk scuttled by with a smile of satisfaction on his fishy face, Oli shrank back behind a pillar. His mind was racing. I now have *two* Subjects, he thought, fishy Subject A and shifty Subject B. Which one shall I follow? He decided on Subject B. Plunk, he reasoned, would probably just return to Professor Vakloff's with the parcel and therefore did not require tailing. Oli hurried out of the bus station in time to see Shifty enter a coffee shop on the other side of the road, but then something else caught his attention. Another man was standing near the same coffee shop, holding a mobile phone. It was Mr Bismuth.

The science teacher seemed to notice Oli at the same moment as Oli noticed the science teacher. He put away his phone and crossed the street.

'Hello, Oli,' he said quietly. 'What are you doing here?'

'Oh, hello, Mr Bismuth,' returned Oli as casually as he could. 'How are you?' he added, playing for time.

'I'm fine, thank you,' replied the science teacher. 'So, what are you doing here, Oli?'

Oli's heart was thumping. There was something in Mr Bismuth's soft voice that he suddenly found oddly menacing. 'I'm . . . I'm checking the timetable,' he said.

'I see,' nodded Mr Bismuth and he rubbed his beard thoughtfully.

'What are *you* doing, Mr Bismuth?' asked Oli suddenly.

'Oh, I was just passing,' he replied. 'Goodbye, Oli.' He turned and walked quickly away.

Oli leant against the bus station wall and let out a deep breath. Then he remembered Shifty and glanced towards the café. Subject B was now seated at the bar. Was it an Assignation, wondered Oli, with Mr Bismuth, perhaps, who had now been forced to leave? Or was Subject B simply waiting for the next bus back to wherever he came from? Perhaps Mr Bismuth's job was to pick up the parcel from Plunk, as an extra-sneaky way of throwing lurking spies (like Oli) off the trail. Oli wished now that he had followed Subject A again. He might be missing the crucial handover because he was lurking in the wrong place, watching the wrong man drink a cup of coffee.

Oli sighed. He had made a real mess of his very first mission and even *The Good Spy's*

Handbook wouldn't be able to help. Or would it? He recalled another tip from that esteemed manual:

Never miss an opportunity to learn more about the enemy!

At least he could make a note of which bus Subject B left on (having been much too excited earlier to notice which one he had arrived on) and meanwhile he could practise his Observation Skills. Oli took out his notebook and started observing.

Subject B, he decided, was a bit taller than Mr Bismuth and a bit shorter than Professor Vakloff. He was about thirty. He had an average build and wore jeans, a black T-shirt and a black leather jacket. He had dark, very short hair, a broken nose and, of course, those shifty eyes. He

ordered coffee, or possibly tea, and Oli noticed
that when it arrived he put two sugars in it and
stirred it with his left hand.

The man glanced at his watch from time to
time and after about twenty minutes he stood up,
withdrew a couple of coins from his pocket and
tossed them on to the table.

Oli melted into the shadows of the bus station
as the man came out of the café and crossed the
street to join a queue of people who were now
shuffling forwards to climb aboard a bus. The
doors clattered shut and, as the bus pulled out of
the station, Oli checked the name on the front:
Bilchester. Then he legged it back to his Secret
Intelligence Headquarters, feeling very pleased
with himself.

7
Footsteps and Shadows

On reaching the High Street, Oli found that the fishman had been replaced by a ghost. It wasn't a very good ghost, just a sheet with eye-holes, but it was probably a lot more comfortable than all that foam rubber and Oli couldn't blame Skipjack for wanting to change.

He went up to the ghost and whispered, 'I followed him to the bus station.'

Skipjack made a sort of grunting noise.

'He went into the waiting room and when he came out again he was carrying a package.'

Skipjack grunted again.

'Are you feeling OK, Skip?'

It was at the third grunt that Oli realised his friend had mysteriously grown by about two inches and was also considerably broader.

'You're not Skipjack!' he cried and, seizing

the sheet, he hauled it off the ghost. There stood Slugger Stubbins. With his cricket bat.

'What have you done with Skipjack?' demanded Oli.

'Nothing.' Slugger glared. 'I'm waiting for him.'

'Here I am!' called Skipjack's voice and the fishman came galloping out of the joke shop. Slugger raised his bat but quickly lowered it again when he saw what Skipjack was waving in the air. It was a £10 note.

'I didn't recognise you under that sheet, Slugger,' said Skipjack. 'I thought you were a real ghost and I was too frightened to come out. Look what I've got for you.'

Slugger held out a hand like the kind a magician would make out of balloons. On it Skipjack placed the £10 note.

'About time,' said Slugger, stuffing the money into his pocket.

'Spend it wisely,' Skipjack told him. He said this because he had a very old and gnarled uncle who came to visit occasionally and who always accompanied the ceremonial distribution of £5 notes with these same words. Skipjack knew from experience, therefore, that being told to 'spend it wisely' took nearly all the fun out of receiving money. He watched with a delighted grin as Slugger lumbered away. 'I wish I could see the look on his face when he tries to pay for something and all he can find in his pocket is a piece of blank paper,' he chuckled. 'He'll be completely mystified.'

'What if he comes back for another tenner?' asked Oli.

'Relax, matey,' said Skipjack airily. 'I've paid for the skeleton now, and the wig, and by tomorrow I'll have earned enough to pay Slugger, too, if I really have to. And Doctor Levity says that if we hire out all twelve monk outfits he'll give me a bonus. Hey, you could wear a monk outfit, Oli.'

'I'm going as a Secret Agent,' said Oli firmly.

'Shame. Maybe Sid will go as a monk. Or a fairy godmother. I'm getting a bonus for those, too. Nobody ever wants to be a fairy godmother. I'm definitely *not* going as a fishman. It's a brilliant costume but it's blogging uncomfortable. I only kept it on for the padding – I thought if Slugger caught me his cricket bat would just bounce off. Let's go inside and you can tell me about Plunk while I change.'

As Skipjack clambered out of his costume, Oli asked, 'Where's Doctor Levity?'

'Gone out somewhere. Daisy's with Tara at your house. Your mum is making their costumes. Tara wanted them to go as leopards and Daisy wanted them to go as fairies so they've met halfway.

'What's halfway between a leopard and a fairy?' wondered Oli.

'A Pink Panther.'

'Of course,' said Oli. 'Listen to this about Plunk. You were right to think he was looking dodgy. I followed him all the way to the bus station.'

'Mr Grimble!'

'I know. Luckily he wasn't around. Anyway, two really suspicious things happened. First, there was a Drop.'

'A what?'

'A Drop. That's what it's called when someone leaves something somewhere and someone else picks it up. A man with shifty eyes got off a bus and left a package in the waiting room and Plunk went in and collected it.'

'Wow! What was the other suspicious thing?'

'Mr *Bismuth* was there.'

'With his beard?'

Oli's eyes rolled. 'Yes, Skip. But that's not the point. All the time I was following Plunk I had this really weird feeling that someone was following me, and when I came out of the bus station, there was Mr Bismuth. So that proves he's involved with Professor Vakloff and Plunk.'

'Double dodgy,' nodded Skipjack.

'He came over while I was watching the shifty man and asked what I was doing there. I came up with an excuse but I know he didn't believe me, especially as he must have seen me following Plunk.'

'So what do you think he was up to?'

'I've got two theories,' Oli told him. 'Theory One: Plunk was going to leave the package for Mr Bismuth in a second Drop somewhere. Theory two: Mr Bismuth had an Assignation with Subject B (that's the shifty guy) in the café which he couldn't keep because I was there.'

'Of course, you know what this means,' said Skipjack. 'The baddies know you're on to them.'

Oli waved an unconcerned hand. It was a hand that had turned so many pages of *The Good Spy's Handbook* that he could quote exactly how the spy world wagged. 'They'll just think I was messing about. Grown-ups never take kids seriously where spying's involved.'

'Or anything else,' agreed Skipjack. 'I still

can't believe that Mr Bismuth is part of a
criminal gang. He's so boring.'

'Silent but deadly,' said Oli, darkly.

Not wanting to miss the fun, Skipjack was also
spending the night at Sid's place. They had a
cosy evening munching pizza in front of the
telly, while behind them Sid did energetic things
with dumbbells. 'If I'm going to beat Herbert
Haystack,' she told them, 'I'll need muscles like
the Incredible Hulk.'

'What, green?' enquired Skipjack.

'Green would be good,' puffed Sid. 'It would frighten all my opponents. By the way, I need someone to look after my pizza stall at the fair during the contest. How about it, boys? I'll pay you.'

Oli shook his head. 'No thanks, Sid. We want to be free to spy on Professor Vakloff. You could ask Tara. She'll do anything for her Running Away to Africa money.'

Before they went to bed, Oli slipped out to set up the trip wire. He had already placed the alarm circuit just inside the joke shop window, which Daisy had promised to leave a little bit open. Now he checked that the triangle of paper was in place between the two ends of the clothes peg and reached in to switch on the circuit. The orange streetlight picked out a huddle of Daisy under a duvet on the floor. She did not stir as Oli picked up the coil of fishing line and, taking care not to tug too hard, began unrolling it.

As Oli crept past Professor Vakloff's front door he tried not to think that unseen eyes might be watching him from behind black windows above. He drew the line taut, about twenty centimetres above the top step, and with very nervous fingers he tied the end to railings on the other side. Then he scampered back to Sid's.

'Ring, please, in the middle of the night,' he ordered the sitting room telephone before he climbed into his sleeping bag, shoved the snoring Skipjack over to his own side of the sofa bed, and went to sleep.

BREEP! BREEP!

Oli reached out to hit his alarm clock, but instead he hit Skipjack.

'Ow!' shouted Skipjack.

What's Skipjack doing in my bedroom? wondered Oli.

BREEP! BREEP!

Now Oli remembered: he was at Sid's place. And that wasn't an alarm clock, it was Sid's telephone! Half in, half out of his sleeping bag, he stumbled across the room and grabbed the receiver.

'Daisy?'

'Yoda's talking!' she squeaked.

'I'm on my way.'

He pulled on his trainers and shook Skipjack, who had gone straight back to sleep. 'Wake up! The trip wire's gone off. Skip – wake UP!'

Skipjack groaned and rolled over.

Oli put his mouth to Skipjack's ear and whispered, 'Slugger's here!'

'What?' Skipjack sat up, wide awake.

'That's better,' grinned Oli. 'Watch the window. And stay awake this time.'

'With friends like you I don't *need* Slugger,' grumbled Skipjack, clambering off the sofa bed.

Crossing the street, Oli saw that a light was now shining from the dentist's ground-floor window, but the blind was pulled right down so he could not see inside. On the pavement near the joke shop door he spotted the little triangle of paper which had been pulled out of the clothes peg, setting off the alarm. Daisy opened the door. Inside the shop Yoda was warning anyone who would listen that he sensed a disturbance in the force. Oli switched off the circuit and took up his listening position against the wall.

At once he heard talking.

'Did you finish it in time?' asked a low voice.

'Of course,' replied Professor Vakloff. 'Everything is ready.'

'And, Plunk, you have the explosive?'

Oli nearly dropped the salad bowl.

'Yes, Big B,' said Plunk. 'Enough to blow up this whole little town, Nya-ha.'

'Control yourself, Plunk,' ordered Vakloff. 'We will use only as much as we need.'

'Yes, master,' said Plunk, sounding disappointed.

'And you must remember to open the windows just beforehand, to let out the blast.'

'Yes, master.'

Oli heard a cough. Then the low-voiced man spoke again. 'Excellent. Let us drink to the success of our mission, gentlemen. The plan cannot go wrong. This time in thirty-six hours we will be far away, and rich.'

Oli heard the clink of glasses meeting in a toast. Then he heard nothing more and he motioned to Daisy to watch from the window in case anyone came out. Soon he heard quick footsteps approaching. Daisy ducked, just as the streetlight threw the shadow of a passing man across the joke shop floor. Oli glanced up at Sid's window and saw Skipjack peeking out, watching the owner of the shadow hurrying away down the street. Then Skipjack glanced back at Professor Vakloff's house, his jaw dropped in alarm and he disappeared. A moment later Oli heard more footsteps, slow and deliberate this time, coming along the pavement towards the joke shop. He leapt up to grab the alarm circuit

from the sill and close the window. Then he
and Daisy pressed themselves against the wall
beneath the window and held their breath. The
footsteps stopped and a new shadow loomed
across the joke shop floor, a long shadow with
enormous ears. After an agonising pause, the
shadow slipped away and the footsteps retreated.
Oli and Daisy were still glued to the spot when
there came a third set of footsteps. The joke shop
door began to open.

Doctor Doom

'Daisy?'

'Grandpa!' cried Daisy and scrambled to her feet.

Doctor Levity flicked the switch by the door and the room was flooded with light. Oli stood up, breathing heavily.

'We thought you were Vakloff,' he said.

Doctor Levity looked appalled. 'I'm very glad I'm not. All that plaque and decay. Yuk.'

Oli noticed that he was carrying a large camera round his neck.

'Where have you

been, Grandpa?' asked Daisy.

'Oh, I went for a walk,' he replied vaguely.
'I couldn't sleep. And, talking of sleep . . .' He
glanced at Oli.

'I'll go,' said the boy. 'Thanks for all your help,
Daisy. See you tomorrow.'

On the pavement outside, Oli looked around
for the triangle of paper but it had disappeared.
Someone, he thought, has gathered up the
fishing line. Little did Oli realise, as he darted
back across the street, that he was being watched
by a pair of sharp eyes.

Upstairs at Sid's place, Skipjack was waiting
for him, wide awake.

'Tell me what you saw,' demanded Oli.

'Tell me what you heard,' demanded Skipjack
at the same time.

So Oli told him and Skipjack's eyes grew
to twice their usual size at the mention of
explosives. 'What are they going to blow up?'

'I don't know,' said Oli. 'I think the plan is to
use it in their own house, because they talked
about opening doors and windows to let out the
blast. Maybe they're building a space rocket in a

secret workshop under the garden.'

Skipjack looked doubtful. 'Or maybe not,' he said. 'How many people did you hear talking?'

'Only Vakloff and Plunk and one more. I didn't recognise the third man's voice, cos he spoke really quietly, but he had a cough that I thought I'd heard before. Did you see him leaving?'

'Yes, but only enough to tell that it was the same person I saw on Monday. The Mysterious Midnight Visitor.'

'Could it have been Mr Bismuth?' asked Oli hopefully.

'I don't think so. Not tall enough.'

'Did you see anyone else leave?'

'No, cos Professor Vakloff came out just after the Mysterious Midnight Visitor and he looked straight up at this window, so I ducked. The next time I peeped out, Vakloff had vanished and the only person I could see was Doctor Levity, going into the joke shop.'

Oli remembered the camera. 'Yes, a bit of a coincidence that he was out, too,' he said, thoughtfully.

Dawn had hardly broken on Friday when Oli was woken once again by the telephone. A moment later Sid came bouncing in holding the handset. 'Morning, Oli,' she shouted. 'It's your mum!'

Oli frowned. What was the point of being independent and going for sleepovers if your mum rang you first thing in the morning? He would get this over with as soon as possible and go back to sleep.

But Mum's first five words put an end to that plan. 'Professor Vakloff has just rung,' she told him. 'He needs to see you again.'

Oli gripped his sleeping bag. 'Why?' he squeaked.

'Apparently there is a National Fluoride Test for eleven-year-olds that he forgot to do during your last visit. It's just a formality. I said we'd go this morning. Don't sound so worried – he promised it wouldn't hurt. I'll call for you in an hour. Enjoy your lie-in.' She hung up.

Oli sank back with a groan. Enjoy his lie-in? How, when he was shortly to be at the mercy of

Doctor Doom? For he had a nasty feeling that this National Fluoride Test was just a ruse to lure him into Vakloff's web. It was time to wake up Skipjack. Oli thumped the neighbouring sleeping bag until a straw-coloured mop surfaced from the top.

'Guess what, Skip: Professor Vakloff wants to see me again. Mum's taking me there in an hour.'

'Great. You can do some more spying.'

'You don't get it Skip. He must suspect something and he wants to scare me off.'

'Relax, Oli. He can't do anything with your mum there. Ask her to go in with you.'

'Good idea,' said Oli, marginally relieved. 'And if he does try something, I can always copy Tara and bite him.'

So sixty minutes later, and for the second time that week, Oli found himself standing on Professor Vakloff's doorstep. He thought he detected an even colder look than usual in the fishy eye of Plunk, but it was hard to be sure. Then came Mum's bombshell.

'I'm just popping over to the bank,' she said.

'I'll be back before the dentist has finished with you.'

So many words of panic rushed from Oli's brain towards his mouth that there was a massive word-jam and all he could do as Mum left was to stare, speechless.

'Oliver Biggles to the surgery, please.'

It was the summons he had been dreading. Oli drew himself up. He still had the Biting Plan.

'Good morning, Oliver,' said Professor Vakloff, as Plunk shut the door behind his patient. 'Sit down.'

With extreme reluctance, Oli approached the big green chair and climbed into it. He felt himself being raised far away from the floor as the chair flattened out. Vakloff tied the strings of his surgical mask and pulled on his long rubber gloves with a snap. The angled light was flicked on and manoeuvred into exactly the spot where it could glare into Oli's eyes.

'Open wide,' said the dentist.

Oli opened his mouth half a millimetre, his eyes alert for the first sign of anything sharp. But Vakloff merely popped a wad of cotton wool into his mouth. Then another. Then another. And then another dozen. Just when Oli realised what was happening and was about to take them all out again, he felt two pairs of metal restraints lock around his wrists and ankles. He struggled and tried to cry out but with a mouth stuffed with cotton wool he could only produce a muffled 'mmmmmmm!'

Professor Vakloff held up an enormous syringe.

'Now, Master Biggles,' he said, 'I want to know why you've been spying on me.'

'Mmmmmmm!' said Oli again (= 'Help!')

'We can do this in one of two ways,' continued the dentist. 'The easy way, in which I remove enough cotton wool for you to talk and you tell me what you've been doing, or the hard way.' He squeezed the syringe slightly so that an arc of liquid squirted out in a glitter of tiny droplets. 'Formic acid,' he murmured, 'distilled from bee stings. Very nasty. I would recommend the easy way.'

'Mmmmmmm, mmmmmmm!' said Oli (= 'Help, help!')

'Assuming that you intend to be sensible, I shall now remove the cotton wool. In case you decide to shout for help, I should warn you that this acid is extremely painful wherever it is injected. I would also, naturally, deny everything to your mother and tell her that I have discovered several teeth which need urgent extraction. Do you understand?'

Oli nodded vigorously and thought fast while the balls of cotton wool were plucked out. His mouth felt like the inside of a bird's nest. He spat out the last woolly strands.

'Well?' demanded Vakloff.

'I haven't been spying on you,' said Oli.

'Don't lie, boy,' hissed Vakloff. 'I've seen you sitting in the room above the pizza shop, watching my house. And last night I found what I can only imagine to be a trip wire.'

'OK,' said Oli, 'I have been spying on you –'

'Ah-ha.'

'– but I've been spying on everyone else in the High Street as well. I'm practising to join MI6, you see.'

Vakloff leaned in with the syringe. 'Tell me

what you've seen.'

'Almost nothing. Just Mrs Higginbottom.'

'My assistant Plunk tells me you followed him to the bus station on Wednesday,' said Vakloff. 'Why?'

'I didn't follow him. I just happened to be going there at the same time. I went to check a timetable.'

'For which bus?'

The word 'bus' always made Oli think of his old enemy Mr Grimble, so he said, 'The Number 11.'

Vakloff's sharp eyes narrowed. 'You think you are clever, Master Biggles. But if I have any more disturbance from you or your weird friend, if I so much as see you in the High Street or find that you have spoken about anything you imagine you have seen here, I shall at once –' he paused, '– tell your mother that you have been skiving your after-school Dance Club to play rugby.'

Oli was stunned. How did he know?

'I am sure,' continued Vakloff, 'that she would be disappointed and angry to know how you have been deceiving her.'

Oli was silent. Then he said, 'I haven't seen anything to tell anyone about.'

'That is because there has been nothing to see,' replied the dentist. He put the syringe down, released the restraints on Oli's ankles and wrists and pushed away the light. Then he lowered the chair, but long before it had come anywhere near the floor Oli had leapt out of it. The last thing he heard as he ran down the passage was the dentist calling, 'Goodbye, Master Biggles,' and laughing an evil laugh.

'Slow down!' cried Mum as Oli ran straight through the waiting area to the front door. She found him outside, leaning against the railings with his eyes closed. 'It can't have been that bad,' she smiled and gave his hair a ruffle. 'Oh, look – is that Skipjack?'

Oli opened his eyes and saw, outside the joke shop, a giant corn-on-the-cob.

'Can I go and tell him something?' he asked.

'Of course. I'll wait here.'

'You look *terrible*,' marvelled Skipjack as his friend approached. 'What happened?'

'It was torture,' Oli shuddered. 'He's not just a dentist, Skip – he's Doctor Doom. I have to lie low. Can you come round to my house when you've finished?'

'I'll get there as soon as I can,' promised Skipjack. Then he saw a cheerful sight – Mr Grimble the bus driver was coming out of the bank. The sight of Mr Grimble was not one that Skipjack usually found cheerful, but he had earlier, on seeing the bus driver going *into* the bank, been struck by a brilliant idea and had been waiting for his reappearance. He bounded up.

Mr Grimble was not at all pleased to be accosted by a 5-foot corn-on-the-cob and even less pleased to discover that inside this enormous vegetable was one of his arch-enemies: Skipjack Haynes.

'Mr Grimble!' panted Skipjack. 'I'm so glad I found you in time.'

'In time for what?' demanded Mr Grimble.

'In time to tell you that there is still one costume left in Doctor Levity's shop for you to hire for the Summer Fair tomorrow.'

'I don't want a costume for the Summer Fair,' growled the bus driver.

'You'll want this one, Mr Grimble,' Skipjack told him.

'Why? What kind of costume is it?'

'A gorilla,' said Skipjack. 'Goodbye, Mr Grimble.'

In the Biggles tree house later that day, Skipjack's eyes grew wider and wider as he heard all the terrifying details of Oli's encounter with Professor Vakloff: the 10-gallon syringe full of formic acid and the steel wrist and ankle restraints, whose sharp edges bit into Oli's flesh as he bravely struggled to free himself. But the thing that most outraged Skipjack was that Vakloff had called him 'weird'.

'How dare he call *me* weird,' he demanded, 'when *he's* the weirdest weirdo in Weirdsville? Let's go right now and tell Inspector Flower.'

'There's a teeny problem,' said Oli. 'Professor Vakloff has found out that I've been skiving Dance Club. He's threatened to tell Mum if we speak to anyone.'

'He's worse than your sister,' said Skipjack.

'I know. What I don't understand,' Oli continued, 'is how he found out. The only person who knows, apart from us, is Tara.'

'But what if we don't tell Inspector Flower and Vakloff blows up the whole town?' asked Skipjack.

'He's not going to blow up the whole town,' said Oli. 'He said so.'

'A little bit of the town? The bit we're in?'

Oli frowned. 'I suppose we could make Inspector Flower promise not to tell Vakloff that he heard it from us,' he said. 'Come on. Let's go to the police station.'

Oli and Skipjack divided grown-ups into three main types: nice ones (who could remember what it was like to be eleven), boring ones (who couldn't) and nasty ones (who wanted to make all eleven-year-olds as miserable as possible). Inspector Flower belonged in the first category. And he played rugby.

Inside the small police station, Constable Bosk was at the front desk preparing Safety Awareness notices for tomorrow's fair. He was happy. He always enjoyed the Summer Fair. It was a day when he could stride about in his uniform and feel very important. He could almost make up the rules as he went along and everyone had to do what he said. Of course, it helped that his uncle was the mayor.

When the door of his police station opened and he saw who was coming in, he frowned. He was feeling much too important to be bothered by a pair of kids.

And when Oli saw who was sitting at the front desk he frowned, too. What he had to say was much too important to tell Constable Bosk.

'We'd like to speak to Inspector Flower, please,' he said.

PC Bosk's frown deepened. 'What about?' he demanded.

'It's a secret.'

The double chin that bulged over PC Bosk's collar wobbled. 'A secret, is it?' he sniffed. 'Well, Inspector Flower isn't here – the mayor gave him a week's holiday. That means I'm in charge of this town and everyone in it, so you can either tell your secret to me or you can take it home again.'

Oli scratched his head. This was tricky. 'Hang on,' he said and turned to Skipjack. 'What shall we do?' he whispered.

'Tell him,' advised Skipjack, 'but make him promise to ring up Inspector Flower straight away.'

So Oli told him. And this is what he said.

'Professor Vakloff isn't a real dentist. He's an International Criminal Mastermind and he's got a plan to explode something tomorrow with his assistant Plunk, who we're pretty sure isn't a real assistant, and someone else called Big B.'

PC Bosk cleared his throat. 'And how do you happen to know all this?' he enquired.

'I've been spying on him,' said Oli proudly, 'with my periscope and my listening device.'

The constable's eyebrows scrunched together in fierce disapproval, but Oli failed to notice this warning sign and asked hopefully, 'So, are you going to arrest him?'

'No, I am not going to arrest him!' spluttered PC Bosk, 'but I might arrest you!'

'Arrest me?' Oli was confused. 'Why?'

PC Bosk stood up and began counting off on fat fingers: 'Spying on innocent citizens, wasting police time, making false accusations and generally disturbing the peace – *my* peace. So, get out – fast – before you find yourself locked up behind bars.'

He marched to the door, flung it open and stood beside it, tapping his foot. Oli and Skipjack got out, fast.

'He didn't even *try* to believe us,' complained Oli.

'He has less imagination than one of Herbert Haystack's turnips,' agreed Skipjack.

They walked on in silence for a while. Oli was mentally replaying the scene in the police station and trying to pin down a niggle that was buzzing about in his head. 'I've got it!' he exclaimed. 'The cough!'

'What cough?'

'PC Bosk's. Did you notice his cough? It was the same cough that Big B coughed in his meeting with Vakloff and Plunk! Constable Bosk must be Big B!'

9

Stink Bomb Calling
Whoopee Cushion

'Constable Bosk – Big B?' said Skipjack
doubtfully. 'But I thought you decided that Mr
Bismuth was Big B?'

'That was before the cough,' Oli told him.
'Also, Mr Bismuth is too tall and thin to be the
Mysterious Midnight Visitor – he must be just
another member of the gang. Constable Bosk
is Big – well, fat – and his name begins with B.
And he's the right shape to be the Mysterious
Midnight Visitor and now – oh, no! I've gone
and told him all our suspicions! He's bound to go
straight to Vakloff!'

'But Constable Bosk is too stupid to be the
leader of a bold and brilliant criminal gang,'
objected Skipjack.

Oli shook his head. 'He's just *pretending* to be
stupid.'

'No one can pretend that well,' said Skipjack. 'But there's one way we'll find out if you're right, and that's if your mum tells you off for skiving Dance Club.'

'That's not a good way to find out I'm right,' groaned Oli. 'Oh, why did Inspector Flower have to be away just now? It's blogging annoying.'

'It's not blogging annoying for the gang,' Skipjack pointed out. 'It's very useful.'

'Anyhow, we're on our own now,' said Oli. 'All we can do tomorrow is wait. When the High Street is full of people for the parade we can slip into Doctor Levity's. I'll watch Vakloff's house from the back and you watch the front and if anything gets blown up we'll ring 999.'

'We ought to have walkie-talkies,' said Skipjack, pleased. 'Let's go and borrow Sid's.'

'But we can't show our faces in the High Street,' Oli reminded him, 'in case Vakloff thinks we're spying again.'

'We can ask Sid to meet us somewhere,' suggested Skipjack.

Oli's eyes lit up. An assignation! Just like in *The Good Spy's Handbook*. When they reached his house they went straight to the phone.

'Hi, Sid! It's Oli here.'

'Hiya, Oli!' Sid's voice came booming down the line. 'How's the spying?'

'That's why I'm ringing. Can we borrow your walkie-talkies?'

'Sure. Come and get them.'

'We can't, cos Professor Vakloff is a bit cross about our spying. So I had to promise him we'd stay away from the High Street.' Sid chuckled. 'Tell you what – I'll bring them to the park. I could do with some fresh air. I'll meet you by the pond in thirty minutes.'

'Thanks, Sid. Bye.'

'Are we going to tell her about your session in the chair with Vakloff?' asked Skipjack. 'And the explosive?'

'No,' replied Oli. 'Cos even though Sid's great, she's still a grown-up. She would only tell us to stay right away.'

The boys were first to reach the pond and they sat down on the grass to wait. They were soon joined, not by Sid but by a troop of optimistic ducks.

'I wish we'd brought bread,' said Oli, looking around. He remembered that he used to come here, years ago, with his mum and Tara, and he was seized by a sudden urge to feed ducks again.

'I wish we'd brought pizza,' said Skipjack, looking up at the clouds. He saw one that reminded him of a slice of Sid's triple pepperoni special and he was seized by a sudden urge to eat again.

A shout of 'Hiya, boys!' made them turn round. Sid was hurrying towards them with a big smile and an even bigger box, flat, white and cardboard.

'Sid!' cried Oli.

'Pizza!' cried Skipjack.

Sid came in to land on the grass, creating a flurry of evasive action among the ducks. She tossed the pizza box on to Skipjack's lap and he opened the lid eagerly.

'Triple pepperoni! And you've even put pineapple chunks and chocolate sprinkles on some of it. Sid, you're awesome.'

'I do my best,' chuckled Sid. 'Well, here they are.' She dug into an orange bag and produced a pair of two-way radios.

'Walkie-talkies!' exclaimed the boys, thrilled. They switched them on straight away and pleasing crackling sounds emitted from the instruments.

'Let's have a conversation right now,' said Skipjack. He pressed the Transmit button, held the radio to his mouth and said, 'Hello?'

But Oli, scholar of *The Good Spy's Handbook*, shook his head. 'You can't just say "hello",' he instructed, 'you have to use code names, like "Broadsword calling Danny Boy" and say "over" when you want me to say something back.'

'OK,' said Skipjack. He looked around inside his head for a pair of code names. Then he pressed Transmit again. 'Stink Bomb calling Whoopee Cushion . . . Stink Bomb calling Whoopee Cushion . . . over.' He released the button and beamed at Oli who grinned and pressed his own Transmit button.

'Whoopee Cushion . . . this is Whoopee
Cushion. Come in, Stink Bomb. Roger Wilco
Out.' He switched off.

'What was all that "Roger Wilco" stuff?' asked
Skipjack.

'I dunno,' said Oli, shrugging, 'but I've heard it
in loads of films and I've always wanted to say it.'

A large orange duck waddled up to Sid and
eyed her boldly, so she threw it a piece of pizza
crust. There was a loud and feathery scrimmage,
from which the orange duck emerged, quacking
triumphantly through a beakful of pizza.

'If ducks were people, that one would be Slugger Stubbins,' remarked Skipjack.

'Talking of Slugger, have you seen him recently?' enquired Oli.

'No,' said Skipjack. 'Good thing I've got such a cunning disguise for tomorrow's fair.'

'I keep telling you, Skip,' said Oli, 'a bananadito is *not* a cunning disguise. It is the most Skipjack disguise in the universe.'

'A bananadito?' repeated Sid.

Skipjack nodded. 'It's like a bandito – you know, big Mexican hat, poncho, moustache. Except instead of guns, I carry bananas.'

Sid chuckled. 'I'm with Oli – he'll spot you in minutes.'

'Not if everyone tells him I'm dressed as the fishman. That's the cunning bit,' said Skipjack. 'I've told Doctor Levity, too, and Daisy and Tara.'

'What's Doctor Levity wearing?' Oli asked.

'He's going as himself,' Skipjack told him. 'He says that's quite exotic enough. But he might have a surprise up his sleeve.'

'A rabbit?' enquired Oli.

Skipjack shook his head. 'That's what I thought, but he says no one is surprised by rabbits any more.'

'Then I wonder what the surprise will be,' said Oli thoughtfully.

10
An Enormous Boom

The day of the long-awaited Summer Fair dawned at last, with cloudless skies promising warmth and sunshine.

Oli had spent the previous evening dreading the telephone and woke up still wondering about Constable Bosk and his Dance Club secret. If, as he suspected, Bosk was Big B, then Vakloff must know by now about Oli's visit to the police station, so why hadn't he carried out his threat and told Mum? Perhaps he was waiting until after the job was done. Oli wondered yet again how his secret could have fallen into Vakloff's spidery hands in the first place, and it now occurred to him that the best way to find out was to ask Tara.

He found his sister in her bedroom where she and Daisy, who had spent the night, were already in costume and painting each other's faces pink.

Oli came straight to the point. 'Tara, have you told anyone about the Silence Money?'

'Yes,' replied his sister, applying a dollop of face paint to the tip her friend's nose. 'I told Daisy.'

'And did you tell anyone, Daisy?' he asked.

'Only Grandpa,' she said.

It was a thoughtful Oli who returned to his own room to put on his Secret Agent outfit. Doctor Levity knew his Dance Club secret. Doctor Levity had also been mysteriously out and about on the night of the tripwire alarm. In fact, Doctor Levity was mysterious full stop. Nobody really knew who he was or where he came from. He was also clever – easily clever enough to be the leader of a bold and brilliant criminal gang. An unwelcome idea was forming in Oli's mind: was Doctor Levity Big B? He was certainly a more likely candidate than Constable Bosk. The policeman was definitely involved in some way; not only did he have the right cough but he matched the shape of the Mysterious Midnight Visitor, whereas Doctor Levity was too tall. But Oli now demoted him from Big B to a mere accomplice. And what about Mr Bismuth? This gang was getting bigger by the day.

Oli's thoughts were interrupted by a loud, 'Hola, hombres!' from the hall below. Skipjack, the Bananadito, had arrived. Oli decided to keep his Doctor Levity suspicions to himself until he had some proof. He fixed his Secret Agent moustache in place, took a last look at his top-to-toe-black Secret Agent reflection, and went downstairs.

'Well?' demanded the bananadito, 'Has your Mum found out about the Dance Club?'

'Not yet,' said Oli in a low voice. 'I think Vakloff's waiting till the job's done. I also think we should keep our mission secret from Doctor

Levity. He might not let us stay behind in the joke shop if he knows there might be a bomb going off. When we get there, I'll pretend I've hurt my back and we'll ask to stay behind for a bit until it's better. Get it?'

'Got it.'

'Good.'

Mrs Biggles dropped the four children at the top of the crowded High Street and then went on to Spiffing Park, where she was helping in the First Aid tent. Sid would be in the park, too, setting out her pizza stall and limbering up for Toss-the-Turnip. The two pink panthers, the secret agent and the bananadito pushed their way through the costumed throng to the joke shop and Daisy used her key to let them in.

'Hi, Grandpa,' she called, but there was no answer. 'He must have gone out already,' she remarked.

Another mysterious absence, thought Oli. He bent down to tie his shoelace and gave a sudden gasp. 'My back! I can't move!'

'You're just pretending,' said Tara with her

usual gentle sympathy.

But Daisy exclaimed, 'Poor Oli! What are we going to do?'

'I don't know,' said Skipjack, who had forgotten this part of the plan and was gazing at his friend in distress. Oli threw him a giant wink disguised as a grimace of agony and Skipjack's face cleared. 'I remember now,' he said. 'It's an old rugby injury. This happens sometimes.'

'No, it doesn't,' said Tara.

'Yes, it does,' said Oli through gritted teeth.

'Can he lie down somewhere?' asked Skipjack.

'Of course,' nodded Daisy. 'Take him upstairs. Here's the front door key. You can follow on when he's better.'

The girls rejoined the crowd outside, leaving Skipjack to help his friend, groaning dramatically, up the stairs.

At 10 o'clock precisely, Constable Bosk blew his whistle and the parade moved away down the High Street. Standing well back from the windows so as not to be seen, the boys watched from the room above the joke shop. They spotted Tara and Daisy, but there was no sign of Vakloff, Plunk or Mr Bismuth.

'They're probably all hiding out next door,' said Skipjack, 'waiting for everyone to go so they can start the Plan.'

'I can't see Doctor Levity either,' said Oli, scanning the crowd of faces. 'I'm going to watch the back. Keep your eyes peeled.'

'Like bananas,' said Skipjack.

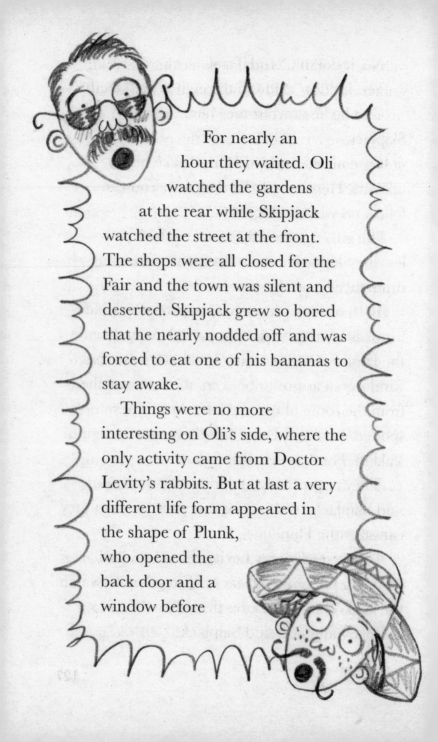

For nearly an
hour they waited. Oli
watched the gardens
at the rear while Skipjack
watched the street at the front.
The shops were all closed for the
Fair and the town was silent and
deserted. Skipjack grew so bored
that he nearly nodded off and was
forced to eat one of his bananas to
stay awake.

Things were no more
interesting on Oli's side, where the
only activity came from Doctor
Levity's rabbits. But at last a very
different life form appeared in
the shape of Plunk,
who opened the
back door and a
window before

vanishing again. Moments later there was an enormous BOOM! Oli was nearly shaken off his feet. As soon as he had recovered, he ran to say 'wow' to Skipjack and the two of them collided on the landing.

'Wow!' exclaimed Oli. 'What was that?'

'An enormous BOOM,' said Skipjack helpfully.

'But what went BOOM?'

Skipjack checked his watch. 'It's 11 o'clock. It must have been the one-gun salute from cannon at the fair.'

Oli shook his head. 'It was much nearer than that. It was Vakloff's explosion. That must have been part of the plan – to set it off at exactly the same moment as the cannon so that it wouldn't be noticed. I'm going next door to see what they're up to. If I'm not out in five minutes and you don't hear from me on the walkie-talkie, go and find Sid.'

'OK, Oli. Good luck.'

Oli ran downstairs and out into the back yard. He peeked over the fence. All was quiet. With the help of a garden table, he climbed over and crept to the open back door of Vakloff's house.

He tiptoed inside. He was in the corridor that led through the house to the waiting area at the front. Along the right hand wall were two doors, both ajar. He knew that the second door led to the surgery. He crept towards the first door and peeped inside.

He was looking into a very ordinary kitchen with a very ordinary floor, in the middle of which was a very extra-ordinary hole. Near the hole was an island-unit on castors, which had evidently been rolled away from its usual position over the hole to allow access. Oli saw that the hole led to a tunnel. He listened for a moment and, when he couldn't hear anything, he lowered himself into the hole.

The tunnel was comfortably big enough to crawl through, its roof supported by wooden posts and crossbeams. This explains all the drilling and hammering and banging, thought Oli. The further he crawled, the darker it grew but the tunnel must have been completely straight because he could see a dim light coming from the far end, about 20 metres away. Where did it lead to? As Oli drew nearer to this light he could see that it came from another big hole. This one had been blasted through a thick, concrete wall. He could hear rustling sounds and low voices. Very cautiously, he popped his head through the hole. He saw a vast steel door and, beyond this door, two people were busy scooping armfuls of money into plastic bin-liners.

Vakloff and Plunk were robbing the bank. Oli watched, agog, as they stuffed wads and wads of notes into the big black bags. It must

be hundreds of thousands of pounds – millions
even. Oli had no idea there was so much cash
in the world. And they were stealing it. And he
could stop them. All he had to do was crawl back
up the tunnel and raise the alarm. Oli began to
turn round, but he dislodged a piece of rubble
and it fell to the tunnel floor with a clatter.

The bank robbers looked up.

'Stop him!' roared Vakloff. Plunk dropped his
bag and lunged forwards. The last thing Oli saw
before he started up the tunnel was the furious face
of this human puffer fish diving towards the hole.

Plunk was surprisingly quick on his hands and
knees and the tunnel seemed to go on for ever.
Oli could sense his pursuer gaining on him and
was beginning to panic when at last he reached
the other end. He scrambled up, hauled himself

out and pulled the island unit over the hole just as Plunk poked his head out.

'Ow!' shouted Plunk as top of head met bottom of unit.

Oli sprinted through the house, out of the front door and into the street.

'Skipjack!' he yelled, screeching to a halt outside the joke shop. His friend pulled open the first floor window and stuck his head out.

'Oli! What's happened?'

'They were robbing the bank!' gasped Oli. 'I've trapped them under a kitchen cupboard!'

'Awesome! I'm coming down.' The head disappeared.

Filled with elation after his adventure, Oli ran into the shop to share a high-five with Skipjack. But the sight of the telephone on the counter pulled him up short. At least one of the imprisoned bank robbers was bound to be carrying a mobile phone and would be able to ring another member of the gang for help. Oli thought fast and by the time Skipjack came tumbling down the stairs he was already on his way out of the shop. 'I'm going to fetch Sid,' he called. 'Phone the police, Skip, and say it's an emergency. And keep a watch for anyone coming to rescue Vakloff and Plunk.'

Sir Henry Widebottom the mayor was at the forefront of the crowd enjoying Toss-the-Turnip when his mobile phone rang. Still smiling professionally, he removed himself slightly from his fellow spectators and answered it.

'Hello? This is the mayor.'

'It is I, Vakloff.'

The smile vanished. 'I told you not to ring me,' he hissed.

'I had to ring you, you silly man. The boy has shut us in the hole. You must come before he fetches others.'

'I can't leave now,' protested Sir Henry.

'If you do not, we will be caught,' said Vakloff, 'and I shall expose you as the ringleader of our gang: Big B.'

Bananas and Bubblegum

Sir Henry swore in a most un-mayoral way and snapped his phone shut. Something had gone wrong with the plan that couldn't go wrong. He summoned his secretary. 'I must leave for a few minutes. I have something urgent to attend to.'

'Shall I order the car, Mr Mayor?' enquired the secretary.

'No.' Sir Henry turned and walked rapidly away, leaving his secretary to scratch a perplexed head. The mayor never walked. And he never had anything urgent to attend to.

When Sir Henry had first seen how many other monks were floating around the fair he had been annoyed. He was the mayor – he didn't want to be dressed like a dozen other people. Now, however, he had good reason to be thankful that he could pass unnoticed through the crowd.

He pulled up the hood of his cloak and hurried away from the fair to the High Street.

As Oli hurried away from the High Street to the fair, he kept a sharp eye out for gang members. Had he not taken the short cut via Smuggler's Alley, his suspicions might have been alerted by the sight of a small monk in a big hurry, but Sir Henry was following the main road because that was the route his driver always took. As the mayor puffed along, he cursed his bad luck. All that careful work organising the roadworks to cover the tunnel-drilling noise and making sure the one-gun salute coincided exactly with the dynamite blast under the bank, and now his brilliant plan was spoiled by a meddling boy.

Down in the tunnel, the bank robbers waited in the semi-darkness. Professor Vakloff sat upright at the bottom of the hole, tapping with long, white fingers the black bag of money on his knees. Plunk was on all fours with his head sticking out of the tunnel. There was a pained look on his puffy yellow face.

'It must be very upsetting for you to see your

perfect plan run into problems, master.'

'Silence, Plunk.'

'I am sure that Big B will soon rescue us and
we will escape and carry out more brilliant
robberies together.'

'Quiet, Plunk.'

'Perhaps we could use the remaining explosive
to blow up Oliver Biggles.'

'Put a sock in it, Plunk.'

'In the meantime, master, I am getting a crick
in my neck from kneeling in this tunnel.'

'You know there is not enough space for us
both to sit in this hole, Plunk.'

'Perhaps master would let me sit on his lap?'

'No, master would not.'

'I understand. I
would say the same
in your position.'

'Plunk?'

'Yes, master?'

'Shut up.'

'Yes, master.'

Skipjack had always, for the whole of his life, wanted to dial 999. And now – finally – he was allowed to, and it was a deep disappointment. The woman at the other end wasn't at all impressed to hear that he and his friend had trapped a pair of bank robbers in a tunnel. She said she would send a patrol car, but she didn't sound in much of a hurry. When Skipjack saw the monk trotting up the High Street, he guessed that the baddies were moments away from being set free and he just knew that the promised policemen would never arrive in time. He would have to stop Vakloff and Plunk himself – but how? He could always dream up brilliant plans when Oli was around, but now his idea-maker seemed to have broken down. What would Oli do? Quote something barmy from *The Good Spy's Handbook* and leap into action. Something like:

ALWAYS WALK BACKWARDS TO LEAVE CONFUSING FOOTPRINTS. IF

POSSIBLE ON YOUR HANDS.

or:

REMEMBER TO CARRY 14 USEFUL THINGS IN YOUR POCKETS, JUST IN CASE.

The monk disappeared into Vakloff's house. Skipjack's hands disappeared into his pockets. These were normally chock-a-block with useful things, but his mum must have had a clear-out because all he could find was a fistful of bubblegum. He also came across his second banana, still in its holster.

How was he going to stop a gang of bank robbers with a fistful of bubblegum and a banana? It was hopeless – or was it? Perhaps enough bubblegum on Professor Vakloff's front steps would glue the baddies to the spot as they came running out? It always worked in cartoons. Skipjack tore open all the little packets and stuffed into his mouth as much bubblegum as it would hold (which was quite a lot).

Down the stairs and out into the street he ran, chewing and chewing until he really thought his jaw would drop off. Then sadly, because he could have blown a record-breaking bubble, he pulled out one stretch of gum at a time, bit it off, rolled it up and dropped it on to Professor Vakloff's top step. When the entire porch was sprinkled with pink blobs he ran round the corner to hide in a side street.

But the first thing Skipjack saw in the side street was Professor Vakloff's car and it occurred to him that, should the bubblegum plan fail, the baddies might use this to make their getaway. That meant he had to find a better hiding place, but it also meant he should try to stop them and *that* meant sabotaging their car. With a banana. What advice would *The Good Spy's Handbook* have now, wondered Skipjack bitterly. The answer came straight back, in capital letters:

NEVER GIVE UP!

In a flash Skipjack knew just what to do. Taking the banana from its holster, he ran to the car and shoved it up the exhaust pipe.

Just in time. He heard footsteps; the robbers

were coming out! Would the bubblegum stop them? Skipjack dived behind a van and waited.

'I must return to the fair at once,' said a voice. 'The absence of a man as important as me will be noticed. Pah! What's this revolting pink stuff all over your steps, Vakloff? It's all over my shoes. Try to get the money to Bilchester without anything else going wrong. I will join you there later.'

A second later, Vakloff and Plunk came tearing round the corner, laden with bin bags. The bubblegum plan had failed. They tossed the bin bags on to the back seat of the car and jumped in. Vakloff started the engine. Skipjack crossed his fingers. The banana plan was brilliant: there was a bang. Skipjack peeped out.

Wisps of black smoke hung in the air. Vakloff
and Plunk were hauling out the bin bags again,
saying loud things in foreign languages which
sounded very rude. Then Vakloff said,

'We shall have to find Big B at the fair and use
his car.'

'But, master,' replied Plunk, 'What if we are
seen by the boy who trapped us?'

'He will not recognise us,' replied Vakloff. 'I
have a plan. Follow me.'

They hurried back to the High Street and
Skipjack, hurrying after them, heard the smash
of glass. He peered round the corner and saw, to
his surprise, that the two robbers were climbing
in through the joke shop window. A moment
later, back through the broken window climbed
two fairy godmothers, complete with wings. One
tall thin fairy godmother in a pink dress and a
blonde wig and one short fat fairy godmother in
a purple dress and an orange wig.

'Doctor Levity's last costumes,' giggled
Skipjack as he watched this odd pair leg it down
the High Street. 'Here's my chance to be a Good
Spy – I'll follow them.'

* * *

Oli had tracked Sid down to the corner of the
field marked out for Toss-the-Turnip, but to his
frustration the contest was in full progress and
he was not allowed near the competitors in case
he was knocked out by a wayward vegetable. A
keen line of turnip chuckers was pitched against
reigning champion Herbert Haystack and, under
normal circumstances, Oli would have enjoyed
watching Sid do battle. But this was not a normal

circumstance. He needed Sid's help and he needed it now, and no amount of jumping up and down or urgent beckoning was getting it.

Sid was touched by Oli's support. There he was, hopping about with excitement and waving. She sent over a big beam and a thumbs-up. Oli groaned. Then all of a sudden Skipjack's voice came crackling out of his walkie-talkie, shouting,

'Whoopee Cushion! It's me, Stink Bomb!'

This brought strange looks from several members of the crowd, so Oli moved a few steps away before replying in a low voice, 'This is Whoopee Cushion. Come in, Stink Bomb. Over.'

'They've escaped!' yelled Stink Bomb. 'First I tried to glue them to Dr Vakloff's steps with bubblegum, only that didn't work. Then I sabotaged their getaway car with a banana! So now they're heading to the fair dressed as fairy godmothers. And look out for a short, fat monk – he's the one who let them out. I think he's the Mysterious Midnight Visitor.'

'Did you ring the police?'

'Yes, but they weren't interested. I don't think they believed me.'

'You follow Vakloff and Plunk,' said Oli. 'I'll find the monk. Out.'

But as Oli looked around the fair he realised that finding the monk was easier said than done. Just from where he was standing he could see eight monks. Even if he ruled out the tall, thin ones it still left too many short, fat ones for him alone to follow. Leaving Sid to challenge Herbert Haystack uncheered, Oli set off to find the pizza stall and enlist some help from the pink panthers.

Sir Henry Widebottom had jogged all the way back to the fair and was on the point of collapse when his mobile phone rang once more.

'Yes?' he gasped.

'It is I, Vakloff. Our car has exploded. We must take one of yours. We are coming for the keys. Where shall we meet?'

'Can't you two bungling idiots do anything right?' shouted the mayor. 'Go to the cake tent. I'll come as soon as this ridiculous turnip business is over.' With the weary sigh of one who is forced to work with nincompoops, Sir Henry returned to the field of battle.

* * *

The word that best describes Tara and Daisy's response to Oli's request for help was 'reluctant'. Tara was reluctant because Sid was paying them extra for every pizza they sold and Daisy was reluctant because, she explained, monks were creepy. Oli tried to explain that the monks at the fair weren't real, but when Daisy insisted that even *pretend* monks were creepy he was forced to give up. As he turned to leave Tara called after him,

'Don't forget it's the Dance Club Show straight after Toss-the-Turnip. Mum's coming to watch and she'll wonder why you're not in it.'

'Well, as this seems to be Don't Help Oli Day, why don't you just tell her why?' replied Oli bitterly as he scanned the horizon for short, fat monks. But he could only see short, fat Constable Bosk, marching about in his uniform and being bossy. This was disturbing because the policeman was the only member of the gang so far who fitted the monk's description, which meant there must be yet *another* accomplice. Oli was just adding up the numbers in the gang so far, and had reached seven, when he spotted one of his chief suspects.

Mr Bismuth was without a disguise but with a beard, and he slipped round the back of a large marquee in what Oli recognised as a Very Suspicious Manner. Ignoring the voice in his head which was quoting *The Good Spy's Handbook* at him:

IF IT LOOKS TOO EASY, IT'S PROBABLY A TRAP!

Oli followed the science teacher behind the tent.

A strong hand grabbed his arm and twisted it round his back. 'I think it's time you told me everything you know,' said Mr Bismuth.

Oli's heart sank. It had been too easy. It was a trap.

12
The Fair and the Ugly

As Mr Bismuth held Oli's arm in an iron grip, a shadow fell across them both from behind and a calm voice said, 'Let the boy go or I'll shoot.'

Mr Bismuth released Oli at once and put his hands in the air. Oli spun round and was astonished to see Doctor Levity, with a *gun*.

'Now, Oli,' said Doctor Levity, 'I think it's time to tell *me* everything you know.'

'Don't tell him anything,' said Mr Bismuth quickly. 'He may be one of the gang.'

Doctor Levity laughed. 'For a man of science, my dear Bismuth, you have a lively imagination. You know perfectly well that I am not in the gang.'

'I could only know that if I was in it myself,' Mr Bismuth pointed out.

'Exactly,' agreed Doctor Levity.

'That's ridiculous,' objected Mr Bismuth.

'Why, then,' enquired Doctor Levity, 'are you demanding information from my young friend?'

'Why, then, are you carrying a gun?' retorted Mr Bismuth.

'Stop!' shouted Oli. 'If you must know, I don't trust either of you – you've both got secrets.' He pointed at Doctor Levity. '*You* disappear in the middle of the night and you are the only person who could have told Vakloff that I was skiving Dance Club and you,' he continued, turning to Mr Bismuth, 'followed me to the bus station and you're wearing a false beard. So there.'

To his surprise, Mr Bismuth began to laugh. 'All right, Oli,' he chuckled, 'you win. But my beard isn't false and my secret isn't what you think. I used to work for the secret service.'

Oli's heart leapt. A real spy? But he kept his cool. 'Prove it,' he said.

'I can't,' replied Mr Bismuth. 'But I recognised Vakloff and Plunk from old cases. Vakloff is an expert safe-cracker from Kalamistan. Plunk is famous in the criminal world for digging tunnels. They call him the Moscow Mole. So when they turned up here, I was naturally suspicious. You'll just have to believe me,' he shrugged, 'or let them get away.'

'I believe you,' said Doctor Levity. He lowered his gun. Oli looked uneasy, but Mr Bismuth said, 'It's not a real gun, anyway.'

'Alas, no,' admitted Doctor Levity. 'It just shoots streamers, see?' He pointed the gun in the air and pulled the trigger. With a loud pop, a multicoloured explosion of paper strings shot out of the barrel. 'Well, dear boy, I am tickled pink

that you suspect me of being a master criminal. I almost wish I was – it would be so exciting. But I'm afraid I am simply an old joke-shop man who was anxious about the safety of a young friend.'

Oli looked from Mr Bismuth to Doctor Levity and suddenly his head echoed with those wise words from *The Good Spy's Handbook*:

TRUST YOUR INSTINCT!

And his instinct told him that they were both goodies.

'Sorry I suspected you,' he said to Doctor Levity. 'Well, here's what's happened. Vakloff and Plunk dug a tunnel to the bank and blew a hole in the wall and robbed it. Skipjack's tailing them here. And there's at least one more member of the gang, wearing a monk's outfit.'

His walkie-talkie started crackling again. 'Oli!' hissed Skipjack. 'They're in the cake tent!'

Oli grinned. 'We're on our way, Stink Bomb. Out.'

Vakloff and Plunk were loitering at the rear of the cake tent, pacing about with their bin bags and waiting for the mayor.

Near the tent pole, meanwhile, Skipjack the banana-less bananadito loitered too, pretending to admire a jam sponge. Pretending so hard, in fact, that he was unaware of Big Trouble approaching from outside, armed with a cricket bat.

'Found you!' yelled Slugger Stubbins and took a mighty swing. Skipjack dodged, but the tent pole didn't. Unequal to the force of Slugger's fury, the spindly pole snapped in two, bringing the whole canvas roof flopping to the ground. Skipjack, whose dodge had brought him near the edge of the tent, rolled out quickly and Slugger, more by luck than skill, appeared seconds later. But Vakloff and Plunk had been by the back wall, surrounded by trestle tables full of cream cakes and custard pies. They had not stood a chance.

'Slugger!' yelled Skipjack as the mad bat boy staggered to his feet and raised his weapon. 'Don't bash me – bash them!' He pointed to two wriggling shapes under the canvas. 'They're bank robbers and we mustn't let them escape!'

'That's a lie,' scoffed Slugger. 'Do you think I'm stupid?'

'Of course not,' lied Skipjack, dashing to the next tent and picking up an armful of prize melons. 'But if it's not true, why aren't I running away from you, huh? Would I stick around and risk being bashed if it wasn't an emergency? I'm sorry about the ten pounds. I'll give you the real money, I promise, but right now I need your help.'

One of the wrigglers had reached the edge of the canvas, where a head now appeared beneath a curly golden wig smothered in sponge and custard. Skipjack lobbed a melon at the head, shouting, 'Take that!' The head retreated. Slugger suddenly saw that Skipjack meant business and, grinning broadly, he set about patrolling the edge of the tent.

'My friend has a cricket bat,' called Skipjack as he went to stock up on more vegetable missiles. 'And he's not afraid to use it. Plus, he's a total psycho, so don't try to come out.' Then he whispered to Slugger, 'Make sure you get them on the bum, not the head, and not too hard. The idea is to keep them here till help arrives, not murder them.'

Slugger nodded. He tiptoed to the nearest wriggler and brought his bat down on the most prominent part halfway along it.

'Ow!' yelled the wriggler.

'This is fun!' snorted Slugger.

Oli and Mr Bismuth hurried towards the cake tent, followed at a more leisurely pace by Doctor Levity, who never hurried anywhere.

'Will you teach me how to be a spy?' asked Oli.

'I wasn't a proper spy,' replied Mr Bismuth. 'I just worked in the lab, inventing stuff.'

'Like Q?'

Mr Bismuth smiled. 'Like Q. But I always wanted to be a science teacher. So I retrained and came here.'

'You can't have known you'd meet someone like Skipjack. He's allergic to science.'

'I'll bring him round,' said Mr Bismuth.

'Have you got any of your inventions with you?'

'Just this.' Mr Bismuth pulled up his shirt

sleeve to reveal a black sports watch.

'Cool. What does it do?'

'Several things. It picks up two-way radio messages, such as "Stink Bomb calling Whoopee Cushion".'

Oli grinned.

As they neared the cake tent, two things surprised Oli: first, it was on the ground and second, Slugger was there, wielding his bat.

'Skip! Look out!' he yelled.

'It's OK – he's on our side,' Skipjack called back. Then it was his turn for a shock as he caught sight of Mr Bismuth. Oli, seeing his face, explained, 'He's on our side, too,' and added in a low voice, 'Mr Bismuth used to invent things for the secret service.'

Skipjack looked at his science teacher in surprise mingled with respect and whispered, 'What about the beard?'

'Real,' sighed Oli.

'Thought so. You can give the tenner straight to Slugger. Did you find the monk?'

Oli shook his head. 'There were too many to follow.'

Mr Bismuth was standing by the collapsed tent with his finger to his lips. Everyone fell silent. The two bumps beneath the canvas were motionless and Oli wondered for a terrible moment if Slugger had been too enthusiastic with his bat and had done to Vakloff and Plunk what he had been threatening all week to do to Skipjack. But Mr Bismuth's silence tactic worked; the two bumps began to inch towards the edge of the tent. Vakloff appeared first and found himself grabbed by the arms and hauled out. He was still holding on to his bin bag of money, which Mr Bismuth tossed aside before drawing from his wristwatch a length of black tape.

'Oli tells me you're anti-science, Skipjack,' he said casually, as he swiftly bound the dentist's arms and legs. 'Here comes Plunk. Someone sit on him.'

'It's more that science is anti-me,' explained Skipjack, as the emerging Plunk found himself unexpectedly being used as a human sofa by Slugger. 'It makes me bibble.'

'That's a shame,' commented Mr Bismuth, moving over to Punk and trussing him up like his master. 'I could have shown you something really

useful, like the formula for stink bombs.'

'That wouldn't make me bibble,' said Skipjack quickly. 'Just think – I always thought stink bombs only *stopped* science. I never knew stink bombs *were* science.'

'See what you've been missing?' Mr Bismuth stood up and viewed his handiwork with satisfaction. The two scowling, cake-splattered fairy godmothers were neatly tied up side by side. 'We'd better summon the police,' he said.

There was, however, no need for this. The tent's collapse, the vegetable hurling and cricket batting and Mr Bismuth's astonishing impersonation of an ancient Egyptian mummy-wrapper had attracted quite an audience and from the back of this semi-circle came the voice of authority.

'Move aside, please. Move aside.'

Constable Bosk had arrived. He eyed the scene with deep disapproval and cleared his throat. 'Now, then,' he said. 'What's all this?'

'It's the remains of a robbery,' Mr Bismuth told him. 'In those black bags you will find most of the contents of the High Street bank.'

Constable Bosk was just puffing himself up to make a suitable reply when an even higher authority parted the crowd: the mayor had arrived.

Sir Henry Widebottom eyed the scene with deep disapproval and cleared his throat. 'Now, then,' he said. 'What's all this?'

'That's just what I asked, Uncle,' declared Constable Bosk, but Sir Henry did not hear him. He was staring at the two bedraggled figures on the ground and now he saw through the wonky wigs, the pantomime dresses and the custard dollops and he realised who they were. He coughed.

And as Oli stared at the mayor, he realised who Big B was. It all made sense: the shape, the cough, the monk's robe and the powerful position. Because only the mayor could have authorised the roadworks which covered the drilling of the tunnel and only the mayor could have made sure to fire the cannon at exactly the right moment to hide the explosion below the bank. Oli longed to shout, 'The mayor is one of the bank robbers!' but he knew that nobody would believe him. He needed proof. His heart was pounding with excitement as he waited to see what would happen next.

Constable Bosk was watching the mayor anxiously. 'Uncle? Are you all right?'

Sir Henry shook himself. 'Explanation, please, Arthur,' he demanded of his nephew.

'This person here,' Bosk told him, indicating Mr Bismuth, 'claims to have foiled a bank robbery. Apparently, those two bags are full of stolen money.'

Sir Henry gazed at the bin liners like a hungry bulldog eyeing up a juicy bone. He even licked his lips.

'Uncle?'

Sir Henry tore his eyes away from the money and nodded vigorously. 'Good work, everyone. Good work. Bank robbers, eh? Take them away. Lock them up.'

Doctor Levity stepped forward from the crowd and to Oli's horror, he picked up the bags of money and handed them to Sir Henry. 'You'd better take these for safekeeping, Mr Mayor,' he said.

'Good idea,' nodded the Mayor, grabbing the bags. But not everyone agreed.

'If you let him take that cash,' growled Professor Vakloff, 'you will never see it again. Tell them who you are, Big B.'

'Big B?' echoed Constable Bosk.

'Big B,' repeated Vakloff. 'Your mayor, ladies and gentlemen, is the man behind this whole robbery.'

There was a low murmur from the crowd.

'This is preposterous!' shouted Sir Henry. 'Are you going to take the word of a common bank robber against me, Sir Henry Widebottom? Take that man away and lock him in prison. I must put this money somewhere safe.' He gripped the bags even more tightly and turned to go.

'Stop!' cried Oli, in desperation. The mayor stopped. Everyone looked at Oli. 'Excuse me, sir,' he said, coming forwards and pointing at Sir Henry's shoe, 'but you've trodden in an enormous dog poo.'

Sir Henry immediately lifted his foot to check his shoe. The sole was covered in pink blobs.

'Bubblegum!' shouted Skipjack. '*You're* the monk who rescued the bank robbers!'

There was another murmur from the crowd, a bit less low this time.

'That's quite absurd,' harrumphed Sir Henry.

'It's not absurd,' insisted Skipjack. 'That's my bubblegum all over your shoe, from Professor Vakloff's front steps.'

'That merely proves that I've been on Professor Vakloff's front steps,' argued the mayor. 'There's nothing criminal about that.'

'There would be something criminal about rescuing bank robbers, though,' put in Doctor Levity. 'Constable, would you permit me to turn out these men's pockets?'

PC Bosk nodded dumbly and Doctor Levity approached the pair of fairy godmothers. He knelt down and, with the curious constable peering over his shoulder, he put his hand inside the pocket of Professor Vakloff's voluminous pink skirt and drew out a crisp new £50 note. While Bosk made tutting noises behind him, Doctor Levity moved on to Plunk and by the same method produced another £50 note.

'I will now look in Sir Henry's pockets,' he said quietly.

Constable Bosk looked nervous. Sir Henry shrieked, 'I absolutely forbid it!' and tried to clutch his robe without dropping the bin bags. But Doctor Levity found his pockets easily and pulled out two more £50 notes. The crowd gasped. Doctor Levity handed the money to Constable Bosk.

'Look at the serial numbers,' he said.

Constable Bosk scrutinised all four notes and cleared his throat. 'The numbers are identical except for the last digit,' he announced. 'They are all from the same batch.'

'I expect they will match the notes which are missing from the bank,' said Doctor Levity.

The crowd clapped. Constable Bosk could only shake his head at the mayor. 'You've been very naughty, Uncle Henry,' he tutted. 'I don't know what Aunt Delia will say.'

'This is all his fault,' shouted the mayor, pointing at Professor Vakloff.

'It was your plan that went wrong,' retorted Vakloff. 'Big B, ha-ha. And you thought it stood for Big Boss. Do you want to know what we called you behind your back? Tell him, Plunk.'

'Yes, master,' said Plunk. 'Big Bottom.'

'Professor Vakloff may be an International Criminal Mastermind,' remarked Oli to Skipjack, 'but he's not very grown up.'

'Neither is Sir Henry,' replied Skipjack, as the mayor stuck out his tongue at his former accomplice.

Just then a loud voice came over the tannoy. 'Attention everybody: The Dance Club Show will be starting in five minutes in the main marquee.'

'Oh, no,' groaned Oli. 'I'm doomed.'

'Nonsense, my boy,' said Doctor Levity comfortingly. 'You couldn't possibly take part now. You are a valuable witness to a major crime. You must go at once to the police station with Constable Bosk and make a statement. I will find your mother and explain all.'

'Doctor L,' sighed Oli, 'you are awesome.'

As they watched Constable Bosk haul Vakloff and Plunk to their feet, Oli remarked, 'It was lucky about Dr Levity finding all those £50 notes. It would have been impossible otherwise to prove that Sir Henry was Big B.'

'How did you know that they would all have stolen money in their pockets, Doctor L?' asked Skipjack.

Doctor Levity smiled. 'Magic, boys. Pure magic.'

13
Loose Ends

Note on Oli's pillow that night:

I just remembered who else knew your Dance Club secret: Professor Vakloff. He was listening on the other side of the fence when I told Daisy in the joke shop yard.

I'm really cross that you've told Mum the truth and it turned out she knew all along. But don't worry - I'll find another way to get silence money.

Tara

Letter from Inspector Flower to Oli and Skipjack, hand-delivered the next day:

Dear Boys,

Congratulations and thank you. You will be pleased to hear that we have tracked down 'Suspect B', thanks to the notes Oli made at the bus station. As you may have guessed, the package he handed Plunk contained the explosive they used to blast through the underground wall of the bank.

We now have all the evidence we need on Vakloff, Plunk and Sir Henry so we will be able to lock them up for a nice long time.

And next time I'm told by a mayor to go on holiday, I shall stay put.

Best wishes,

Inspector Flower

PS Constable Bosk says he's truly sorry he didn't believe you. He's very polite and humble now – having a criminal for an uncle instead of a mayor has improved him enormously.

Headline in Monday's local newspaper:

Photography Competition

The winner of the Summer Fair Photography Competition was Dr Hamish Levity, for his beautiful series of photographs, 'Badgers at Night'. Dr Levity told our reporter that he had taken the pictures on night-time walks to help him sleep.

Another headline in Monday's local newspaper:

New Toss-the-Turnip Champion!

Herbert Haystack was defeated for the first time in twenty years after a thrilling competition on Saturday. New champion Sid Stringfellow said of her victory, 'It all comes of eating lots of triple-pepperoni pizza with extra cheese.' Asked why she had painted herself green for the event, Sid explained, 'It was so I would feel like the Incredible Hulk. But I'll give a free pizza to anyone who can get my hair back to normal.'

The biggest headline of all in Monday's local newspaper:

Bank Robbery Foiled!

A daring attempt to rob the High Street Bank, masterminded by none other than Mayor Sir Henry Widebottom, ended in a dramatic showdown at the Summer Fair on Saturday. Brave local boys Oli Biggles, Skipjack Haynes and Slugger Stubbins tracked the robbers to the cake tent and kept them there until help arrived.

Sir Henry and his fellow conspirators Vladimir Vakloff (known to the boys as Doctor Doom) and his assistant Plunk are now safely behind bars. When asked how he came to suspect the criminals, modest Oli Biggles said, 'It was nothing, really. Anyone could have done it, as long as they had read *The Good Spy's Handbook*.'

Follow Oli and Skipjack in more Tales of Trouble!